LINCOLNSHIRE COUNTY COUNCIL — LIBRARIES

This book should be returned on or before the last date shown

S.

e

M.E.B.

Tom

SO2 2/95

LIBRARY SERVICE TO CENTRES

31 74

D0545679

— 37

— 61

280

58

61

107

184

283

74

177

07. JUL

04. NOV

—4. AUG. 2004

3/99

BUCKLAND COUNT

10 DEC 10.

52

V. DAV.

04. FEB 1

V.R.
D.R.

05. APR 1

30.
24. FEB 1

18. JUL. 2000

31. MAY

24. MAY 1

25. NOV 11.

14. SEP

F DURMAN

The twain shall meet

LARGE PRINT   £6.50

L 5/9

AD 01976308

SPECIAL MESSAGE TO READERS

This book is published by
THE ULVERSCROFT FOUNDATION
a registered charity in the U.K., No. 264873

The Foundation was established in 1974 to provide funds to help towards research, diagnosis and treatment of eye diseases. Below are a few examples of contributions made by THE ULVERSCROFT FOUNDATION:

A new Children's Assessment Unit
at Moorfield's Hospital, London.
•
Twin operating theatres at the
Western Ophthalmic Hospital, London.
•
The Frederick Thorpe Ulverscroft Chair of
Ophthalmology at the University of Leicester.
•
Eye Laser equipment to various eye hospitals.

If you would like to help further the work of the Foundation by making a donation or leaving a legacy, every contribution, no matter how small, is received with gratitude. Please write for details to:

**THE ULVERSCROFT FOUNDATION,
The Green, Bradgate Road, Anstey,
Leicester LE7 7FU. England
Telephone: (0533)364325**

THE TWAIN SHALL MEET

Sharon loves working for Nicholas and Kate, and despite her fondness for Kate, loves Nicholas. Nicholas adores the beautiful Kate and is desperate to marry, but Kate is quite happy with their unmarried state. Sharon suggests that maybe Nicholas should make Kate jealous — but are her motives entirely honourable? Will the plan work? A visit to East Berlin changes everything — for Nicholas, Kate and Sharon.

HILDA DURMAN

THE TWAIN SHALL MEET

Complete and Unabridged

LINFORD
Leicester

First published in Great Britain in 1984

First Linford Edition
published March 1993

Copyright © 1984 by Hilda Durman
All rights reserved

British Library CIP Data

Durman, Hilda
    The twain shall meet.—Large print ed.—
Linford romance library
I. Title II. Series
823.914 [F]

ISBN 0–7089–7331–0

This book is printed on acid-free paper

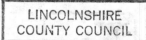
LINCOLNSHIRE
COUNTY COUNCIL

Published by
F. A. Thorpe (Publishing) Ltd.
Anstey, Leicestershire
Set by Words & Graphics Ltd.
Anstey, Leicestershire
Printed and bound in Great Britain by
T. J. Press (Padstow) Ltd., Padstow, Cornwall

Read. 1 ~~Reading~~

KATE DARCY stretched and gave a sigh of delicious contentment. She turned her dark head on the silk pillow to look at her equally dark companion and gave him a dreamy smile. The smile of a woman who has been completely and satisfactorily loved.

He let the back of his fingers stroke gently from the tip of her ear down the side of her face and neck. "M'mm," she murmured, with her eyes closed.

She could easily have fallen asleep, and always felt this way after sex. The telephone shrieked out just as she was drifting away.

"Oh, drat!" she said, without opening her eyes.

It continued to ring out, so with an exclamation of annoyance she reached out for the receiver, pulling the silk bedcover over her nakedness.

Nicholas Andrews smiled at her action. So modest, yet she had given herself to him with complete abandon a short time before.

With his arm behind his head he admired her smooth back as she chatted on the telephone. She had the most gorgeous body of any girl he had known. Her brown eyes were the most remarkable he had ever seen. They were like soft velvet. They could flash with anger, sparkle with enthusiasm, look dreamy and sexy, be filled with sympathy. He had seen her in all these moods. He loved Kate. She gave him great happiness. Only one thing marred this happiness. Kate refused to marry him.

The phone call was obviously of importance so he slipped out of bed, gathered his clothes and went off to the bathroom. When he emerged shortly afterwards Kate, having showered, was clad in brief, lacy underwear, searching through her wardrobe.

"That was Sharon," she said, with her back towards him. "Lord Marston called and wants us to go over to the Hall as soon as we can to make a definite offer for that George III tableware."

Kate was no longer dreamy looking, she was alert and business like as she took a black silk chiffon dress from its hanger and slipped it over her head.

"Oh, yes," he said, watching her flick her hair out with a brush. What luxurious hair she had. "You've already made him a tentative offer?"

"I offered him three thousand for the lot. I reckon we should be able to sell it in separate lots for about five. You are coming?"

"Of course," he said.

"We'll call in the gallery on the way," she said. "I made a list of the stuff and I've left it there. Lord Marston has a fantastic selection. But he only wants to sell a few pieces."

Soon they were gliding through the traffic in Nick's Mercedes which he drove with skill, and arrived at the gallery where the most fabulous antiques were on display.

As they entered the gallery their secretary-cum-assistant watched them come towards her arm in arm, their faces aglow. She knew what they'd been up to. Could tell by the languorous tone of Kate's voice as she answered the phone earlier. In mid-afternoon too. Lucky Kate, thought Sharon, looking at Nick with unconscious adoration. How wonderful to have a tall, virile man like Nick to make love to you. And where would you find another girl like Kate? No wonder he thought she was marvellous.

"How's Sharon?" he asked, flicking the end of her fair hair, just as fair as Kate's was dark.

Kate had gone into the office and returned before Sharon had time to answer him. Now she stood beside him and held out the list for him to see the items for sale and how she had estimated the value of each item.

"Fair enough," he said. "Have you got the cheque book?"

She looked in her bag to make sure and then they were ready to set off to the famous Marston Hall which was almost an hour's driving away from their London gallery.

If anyone wanted to know anything about antiques Kate Darcy was the person to go to. Her father, Sir John Darcy, had been a collector for years, also his father before him, and she had inherited their love for the art of bygone days.

She visited all the big cities in search of the rare and exquisite. Specialising in porcelain, she was nevertheless an expert on silverware, glassware, bronze, copper, and had bought and sold furniture in all periods. She had put on antique displays for members of the royal family, and had bought and sold antiques for them.

Only a couple of weeks ago she had sold a George II mahogany serpentine commode for nearly two thousand pounds which she had picked up for a song at an auctioneers.

"Clever girl," Nicholas had told her, but he was just as good in business himself.

Kate had met Nicholas through her work for he too was an expert on antiques. It had been as much his idea as Kate's to open the gallery for though they did most of their deals privately, they were able to pick up treasures on their travels which justified the opening of an antiques business.

Often in the past Kate and Nicholas had been bidding against each other at private sales, or at sales by auction, and eventually they decided to work together. What Kate didn't know Nicholas probably did, and when they weren't sure they studied the subject together until they were.

Marston Hall was a beautiful building dating back to the seventeenth century. There was a black and white lodge at the entrance marking the beginning of a drive which was lined on both sides with lime trees through which one caught glimpses of lovely parkland.

Nicholas stopped the car and took Kate's hand in a firm grip as they went up the stone steps to the main entrance. A manservant invited them to enter. They followed him through the great hall until they reached the richly decorated salon where they were asked to take a seat while he informed Lord Marston that they had arrived.

"This beautiful building has a soothing effect on me," said Kate. "I felt it the last time I was here."

Lord Marston came along to welcome them and took them to join his wife in the splendid drawing room. Lady Marston was much younger than her husband, an elegant lady, slim and fairly tall.

"You will dine with us when you have finished the business on hand?" she asked.

"Yes, you must stay," urged Lord Marston. "We have some guests coming soon and they'll be pleased to talk to you about antiques. You might find you can do a bit of business with them, too."

They went to complete their business deal first. There were twelve George III dinner plates for sale with gadroon borders, sideboard dishes of later period and other items including an oval dish, octagonal entree dishes, and an oblong shallow bacon dish, all dating from seventeen eighty to eighteen hundred.

They were in perfect condition but Nicholas studied them all very carefully, satisfying himself that there were no skilful repair jobs done which might escape their notice.

His eye fell on a George IV mustard pot with a small shell thumbpiece and leaf capped handle. He examined it carefully and saw that it was made by Pearce and Burrows and was dated eighteen-twenty-seven.

Nicholas noticed Lord Marston's eye on him. "How much for that?" he asked.

"It's not for sale."

Nicholas smiled. "I'll give you thirty for it."

"I'll take forty."

"Thirty five," grinned Nicholas.

"Thirty seven fifty."

"Right," said Nicholas, "that's if it's in perfect condition."

It was and he was pleased to add it to the other pieces. He and Kate never missed any opportunities whether the rewards were great or small. Kate was happy about this purchase. She felt confident of selling most of it to a Mrs Blackham, the wife of a midland industrialist.

Their business concluded, Lady Marston came along and announced that dinner was about to be served so they went with her and her husband to the long dining salon where several other guests were already being shown to their places.

In the early hours of the morning Nicholas stopped his Mercedes before the luxury apartments where Kate lived. She knew he would expect to be invited to spend the night with her, but she wanted to be alone now. Kate often felt a need for her own company and so she didn't invite him in; he never stayed with her at night unless he was asked.

"I'm dreadfully tired, Nick," she said, and he took the hint immediately.

"So am I, pet. I'm ready for my bed. See you tomorrow."

He gave her a kiss and she felt mean as she watched him drive away.

She let herself in. Her flat was completely modern. Fond as she was of antiques there were none here. She believed they belonged in their proper setting and that was not in a modern place, but in stately homes or large country mansions.

She loved her apartment and loved equally the stately home where she had been born in Sussex. It was an Elizabethan house of great charm. The gardens had been laid out later by Capability Brown and were still as delightful today, with velvet lawns flanking the house, which contained some of the most beautiful treasures imaginable.

Weary, but feeling that she and Nicholas had done a good day's work, she kicked off her shoes and went straight to bed, still feeling rather woozy from the wine.

She hung up her dress but scattered her undies about, letting them fall where she cast them off and soon she was fast asleep in her luxurious bed with its silk covers and pretty silk pillow cases.

Sharon Moore was also fast asleep in her little bed in much more humble surroundings. She had not fallen asleep as easily and contentedly as Kate. She was twenty-one, four years younger than Kate, who had employed her since she left school because she had been pleased with her quiet manner and good appearance. There was an air of refinement about her. Her fair hair always looked freshly shampooed and curled delightfully and naturally. She had clear blue eyes, which often looked green, and she looked you straight in the eye as she spoke to you.

Often Kate handed clothes to her for she discarded them after very few wearings, wishing to appear different each time she met clients. "It is important to look as elegant as the people with whom I am doing business," she said, and though Sharon was exceedingly grateful to Kate for handing on her clothes, there were seldom occasions when she could wear them.

If she accompanied Kate, as she was often called upon to do, she felt it appropriate to be dressed smartly but not as glamorously as Kate. A secretary was not there to attract attention. She did not have to create an image whereas Kate must always appear as the wealthy young society girl dabbling in antiques, which indeed she was, in a big way.

Sharon had taken the job in the gallery intending to stay there only until she had finished her studies in shorthand and typing, attending nightschool for this purpose. When she was qualified Kate had discovered what a capable lady she was and had made her a secretary assistant, to be relied upon during her absence, and had increased her salary accordingly.

Sharon would have been able to afford a better place to live and save for her future had it not been for the fact that her father had been seriously injured in a car crash involving a drunken driver. He had received severe spinal injuries which necessitated her mother giving up her job to care for him, and Sharon felt it her duty to contribute something to them until the compensation claim had been settled.

It had been decided that she could be more helpful keeping on her well paid job and sending part of her salary to help them out rather than going home to help her mother cope with an invalid husband.

Sharon didn't want to give up her job. She thought a great deal of Kate and Nicholas and couldn't have found better employers anywhere. Kate treated her more as a friend than an employee and when Nicholas had been away on business was glad of Sharon's company at times. She would invite her to her luxury flat or take her out to dine.

Sharon appreciated Kate's friendship. Their backgrounds were entirely different but Kate never made her feel aware of this. She was most generous, often bringing little gifts for Sharon to brighten up her flat, saying she'd picked it up for a song so that Sharon wouldn't feel too indebted to her.

They had confidential little talks and Kate had told her that Nicholas wanted them to be married. "But for some reason I keep putting him off," she had told her. "I can't think what's wrong with me. He's the nicest man I know, have ever known, yet something holds me back from becoming his wife."

"He obviously adores you," said Sharon, knowing they lived as man and wife almost. In the circumstances Sharon couldn't understand her reluctance to marry Nicholas.

"I know you think I'm an idiot," Kate had declared, "but I have a feeling inside me that I haven't yet met the man with whom I shall settle for the rest of my life."

"Does Nicholas know that?"

"No. I've never told him. I wish the feeling would go away. I want to make Nicholas happy." Sharon believed Kate. She wouldn't deliberately hurt anyone, but it seemed strange that she could be so close to Nicholas and yet refuse to marry him.

Nicholas teased Sharon, treated her as a very young girl. She was sure he didn't realise she was twenty one and when he touched her, playfully gave her bottom a pat as he passed, he didn't realise the effect he had upon her.

She would have given anything in the world to be in Kate's shoes, but she would never win a man like Nicholas. Not a girl like her.

2

AFTER a busy week in the gallery Sharon was looking forward to Sunday and a rest, but she remembered that Kate had asked her to type out an article for her about antiques for a glassy magazine.

She and Nicholas were in the office going through the week's takings. Sharon knew they'd be pleased for they had had a lot of tourists from the Continent buying from them. She was sure Kate would understand why she had had no time to attend to her typing.

They offered Sharon a lift to her flat, as they often did if they were there at closing time, and Sharon apologised for not getting the typing done. "I know it was urgent," she said. "I'll do it tomorrow. I shan't get any interruptions away from the gallery."

"Oh, you mustn't work on Sundays," said Kate. "Supposing we take Sharon with us tomorrow to my home, Nicholas? You wouldn't have to bother getting any meals, Sharon, and you could type it in Daddy's study. We could pick her up on the way, couldn't we, Nick?"

"Of course," he agreed.

Sharon was delighted. It would be wonderful to see Kate's home which she knew was beautiful, yet she felt a little in awe of meeting her parents. She spent Saturday evening shampooing her hair and decided to wear a lightweight suit in midnight blue which Kate had given her and hoped Nicholas wouldn't recognise it as Kate's. "But he won't be looking at me when Kate's there," she told herself.

They called for her early, looking as happy as a honeymoon couple, and Sharon didn't need to be told that they'd spent the night together.

Nicholas drove at a good speed and it wasn't long before they were in the pleasing countryside surrounding Kate's home. They passed an assembly of small cottages of local flint and mellow brickwork, some of them seventeenth-century or even earlier.

When Sharon had been at school they had several times been taken to see stately homes and she had kept them in her memory. Now as they approached the beautiful Elizabethan house where Kate had been born and reared she couldn't believe she was actually visiting as an invited guest and not as a paying tourist.

Many stately homes do not give the impression they have been lived in, but Kate's home had a very warm atmosphere in spite of its grandeur.

Nicholas was obviously a frequent visitor here for he was welcomed cordially by the servants and also by Sir John and Lady Darcy. He seemed quite at ease, but Sharon felt like a Cinderella, absolutely out of place in such a grand house.

She was overawed by the beautiful

paintings, fine panelling, numerous works of art of all descriptions, and terribly impressed by the great staircase and the spacious gallery.

She was introduced to Kate's mother who was a charming lady, and then to her father who seemed very stern, but Kate didn't seem at all affected by his manner.

Kate explained that they had brought Sharon with them because she was going to do some typing for her. "It isn't a big job so I thought we'd bring her along and then she can enjoy herself when she's finished."

After some light refreshment Sharon was taken to Sir John's study and though she had considered him a very stern man he was most courteous and concerned that she was comfortable and had all she required when she sat at his desk.

In a way Sharon was glad to be shut away on her own in the study for she felt almost afraid to move in case she should do some damage.

She sat for a while gazing out of the long windows across glorious parkland. She saw Kate and Nicholas arm in arm going for a stroll, with a couple of dogs bounding around them, excited and full of life. She heard a terrific screech and nearly jumped out of her skin, and then realised it was a peacock when she saw the bird strutting across the terrace.

She began to sort out the papers she had with her in order to start the typing. As Kate said, there wasn't a great deal and it took little more than an hour to finish it. For a long time she sat, unable to find the courage to go looking for Kate to tell her she'd finished and ask her to check it.

It was Sir John who came and found her sitting there. "I didn't like to think of you shut away in here working on a nice day," he said, "Come along, my dear, I'll show you around."

She found him a most charming man and wondered why she had thought him stern and unapproachable. By the time the mid-day meal was announced he had taken her on a tour of inspection.

They met Kate and Nicholas coming back from their walk and Sharon felt that Nicholas was looking a little put out. There was a difference in him somehow to the way he had appeared earlier on. Now he seemed a little cool with Kate, but Kate didn't seem to be aware of it, or was ignoring it.

"I've finished your article, Kate," said Sharon.

"Good. I'll take a look at it after lunch. See if it wants any alterations."

Throughout the delicious meal Nicholas hardly spoke, but Kate had plenty to talk about, telling her parents how well she and Nicholas were doing in business, and listening to all the news her parents had to tell her.

"The Louviers are in England," said her mother. "They have called to see us once and said they'd try and call again today when I told them you'd be here. They're returning to France in a day or so."

"Oh, I do hope they come," said Kate. She turned to Nicholas. "They are charming people. They live in a most gorgeous chateau in the Loire Valley."

"You've stayed there?" he asked.

"Several times when I was a child. The chateau is a small one in comparison with many in that region, but it's like something out of a fairy tale. Its almost hidden in a pine forest. It's fantastic, isn't it, mother?"

"It really is," said Lady Darcy.

Sharon saw that Kate and her mother were very much alike. She supposed Lady Darcy must have been quite as beautiful as her lovely daughter when she was younger, and Sir John obviously adored both of them.

After they'd filled themselves with good food Kate said she'd better look at the typewritten article before the Louviers arrived. "Want to come and read it?" she asked Nicholas.

"Yes, I'll come," he said, but Sharon had the feeling he was still upset with Kate over something. But he read her article carefully and told her it was excellent. "No need for any alterations," he smiled at Sharon. "I expect that's a relief, isn't it?"

"I'm sure it is," said Kate. "You can enjoy yourself now. I'll go and, get some large envelopes and it can be sent on its way."

She dictated a short letter to go with it. "Perhaps you'll slip that into the publisher's office for me tomorrow, Nicholas?"

"Will do," he promised.

They left Sharon to type the letter and address the envelope, and when she'd finished she went to stand by the window looking out across the landscape as Nicholas had done a short time ago. She saw him and Kate standing by a waterfall which came cascading down the rocks of an artificial lake.

She saw the breeze gently lifting his hair and it filled her with a strange yearning. How she envied Kate as she had done so many times in the past. Kate had everything.

She saw her playfully let two fingers walk along the top of his arm, across his shoulder to his neck. He stood without moving and her fingers travelled to the nape of his neck and then moved caressingly through his thick dark hair.

Kate had aroused him as she had obviously intended to do and he suddenly took her hand and gripped it firmly. He turned her round to face him and she lifted her arms to fasten them behind his head. Then Sharon watched as he bent to give her a breathtaking kiss. She wondered how they could possibly kiss for so long without gasping for breath. She was almost gasping for them.

It thrilled her to see Nicholas kissing Kate. What would it have done to her if he had been kissing her instead?

He was about to kiss Kate again when a car appeared on the drive which they saw as soon as Sharon did. Kate said something to Nicholas and he produced a white handkerchief which she took from him and proceeded to wipe away lipstick traces from his mouth, laughing as she did so. And then they turned to greet the elegant looking couple as they pulled up close to them and got out of the car. They had obviously witnessed Kate's action and were laughing as they greeted them.

Sharon guessed these were the Louviers. They had a French air about them, she decided, though she couldn't have said exactly what a French air was. They both embraced and kissed Kate, were introduced to Nicholas, and the foursome were chatting away animatedly as they approached the house to enter.

Sharon began to wish she was in her own flat where she could feel at ease. She realised she couldn't stay here for the rest of the day and yet she was too shy to emerge. Kate wasn't so thoughtless as to leave her for long.

She soon came breezing into the study and said, "Sharon! I *am* neglecting you, dear. I'll sign that letter and then you must come and meet our friends, you'll love them."

And so Sharon was taken to meet Yvonne and Paul Louvier who were with Kate's parents, and found herself being treated as a friend of Kate's rather than as a secretary.

As Kate had said, the Louviers were absolutely charming and she loved listening to them speaking in almost perfect English with such a fascinating accent. Madame Louvier was much younger than Sharon had expected. Probably not more than forty. Very chic and slim. Her dark hair was taken back severely but she still managed to look beautiful for her face had a perfect bone structure and her eyes were even darker brown than Kate's, they seemed almost black. Her deep lilac coloured dress was deceptively simple and Sharon was glad she had decided to wear the smart summer suit Kate had given her.

She was drawn into the conversation and if they sensed her shyness they didn't make it apparent. She told them about her father's accident and they talked about the large number of road accidents they had in France too.

The Louviers accepted an invitation to stay for the evening meal and they dined in the small dining room as they'd done at mid-day, but the Darcys had obviously given instructions to their staff to be prepared for visitors for an exquisite meal was set before them.

"I would love to write a book about your chateau, Yvonne," said Kate, "for I was so fascinated by its historical background and the treasures it contains, I'm sure it would all make wonderful reading. And then there are the vineyards connected with the chateau and your marvellous wines."

"Well why not write one," said Yvonne. "Come and spend a holiday with us. Bring Nicholas and Sharon, we'd love to have you, and would put all the information you require at your disposal. We can provide illustrations and let you see old documents."

"Yes, do," said Paul, enthusiastically.

Kate turned to Nicholas. "Would you help me write a book, darling?"

"If you want me to, but I'm sure you'd be capable of writing it without my help, though you'd need Sharon to type it for you."

Sharon couldn't believe she was being included in this wonderful invitation to stay in a real chateau. But she was, for Kate was accepting the invitation for all three of them. It was marvellous.

Before the Louviers left they all took a walk in the grounds and Sharon was delighted. She would have been disappointed if she had left without seeing more of the exterior.

Sharon wondered why Kate preferred to live in noisy London when she could live here. They saw a most beautiful sunset and Sharon realised that such splendours were missed in built-up areas where high buildings completely hid the glory of the sun sinking in the west.

They reached the house just before the sun had sunk right out of view in a blaze of glory, few stray birds were making swift flight to their nests before it became quite dark.

Before they left, the Louviers made definite plans for the visit to their chateau and they made it obvious they were looking forward to seeing them.

When they were leaving, Sharon noticed that Lady Darcy gave Nicholas a kiss before he left and a very thoughtful look. She seemed fond of him and would no doubt have accepted him as a son-in-law quite happily if only Kate would accept him as a husband.

As they were travelling back to London very little was said by Kate or Nicholas. Sharon knew that Kate was probably tired for it was late, but she had a feeling that Nicholas was more than tired. Perhaps he was disappointed at the way the day had turned out. He could have been hoping that on this visit to her parents Kate would agree to announce their engagement, but it was evident that she was not ready to do so.

They left her at her shabby little place and she was back to reality. The Darcys and the Louviers and Nicholas lived in a different world to hers. One she felt sure she could never get used to.

When she got to bed she went through the events of the day and went to sleep thinking of Kate and Nicholas kissing by the side of the lake, and imagining Kate and Nicholas lying side by side in her apartment.

When Nicholas arrived at Kate's apartment he didn't wait to see if there would be an invitation to stop with her. He wasn't satisfied with the way things were going. He told Kate she was using him just to give her sexual satisfaction but she had refused to let him discuss marriage with her and her parents, although she had insisted there was no one else she cared for as she did him. Nicholas couldn't understand her, and neither could she understand herself.

She supposed one day she would agree to become his wife, but not yet. She wanted to get married, of course, and there was no reason at all why she should keep putting Nicholas off. They had a wonderful partnership and yet she had refused him once again.

"We will marry someday," she told him. "But not yet."

He was hurt, she knew, and he was the last person in the world she would want to hurt, so what was wrong with her?

3

IF Nicholas didn't stay the night with Kate he usually gave her a ring early in the day to see what was on the agenda, but today he didn't and Kate felt very unsettled. She knew he wasn't happy about their present arrangement and it was rather mean of her not to make their relationship more stable. When a man wanted to live with a woman without marriage he was often condemned as simply wanting a sexual relationship and nothing more. Nicholas was not like that. He was thirty four and said it was time he was settled down and starting a family.

"If you don't want to marry me, Kate," he had argued, yesterday, "you don't love me as I love you."

"How can you say that!" she had cried. "I've never been with any other man since I've known you."

"Well why don't you agree to marriage?"

"I don't know," she had declared. "I suppose I want to feel that I belong to myself."

"I wouldn't be possessive," he had assured her and she had smiled. "In that case why can't you be happy as we are?" and teasingly she had added, "you know I don't deprive you of love, darling."

She knew he was deeply affected by her refusal to arrange a wedding date and now he hadn't phoned her as he usually did. Perhaps he was coming straight to her flat for she dialled his number and there was no reply, and she settled with a magazine while she waited.

At last, in a temper, Kate stormed out of her apartment, picking up her own car keys and deciding to go to the gallery on her own. She had wasted a great deal of the morning and was furious and usually Kate was very even tempered. It took a lot to make her angry.

Her car was parked in her garage at the back of the apartments. She didn't use it much these days. It was a white Triumph and soon she was on her way to the gallery feeling none too pleased with Nicholas.

When she arrived Sharon informed her that Nicholas had been and gone and she saw that that infuriated Kate.

"Did he leave any message?"

"He said to tell you he'd delivered your article, and was going to be busy."

"Didn't he say whether he would be returning here or to my place?"

"No. He only called for a few minutes and said we needed more stock and then left."

For the rest of the day Kate was like a fish out of water. She couldn't concentrate on any thing, not knowing whether Nicholas intended to get in touch with her or not. She couldn't plan to do anything herself. Kate often

34

chatted to clients about antiques which was all good for business but today she didn't put herself out at all and left early.

Sharon kept thinking about her and Nicholas. Both were miserable, she could tell, and yet when they were happy together you couldn't find a more delightful couple. Perhaps Nicholas should neglect Kate now and again, she thought. It might make her appreciate him more and want to be married to him.

For three days she didn't see them together and wondered if Nicholas had actually decided to finish with Kate completely. He didn't come to the gallery and Kate hung about as if waiting for him to put in an appearance. One morning when Sharon went to the gallery there was lots of new stock and a list giving all the prices and listing information about some of the pieces. So Nicholas was working even if he wasn't seeing Kate.

It would be a shame if the partnership

ended. Sharon had watched the two together with envy and couldn't imagine they could part and not see each other again.

Kate missed Nicholas more than she cared to admit. She supposed this could be his way of trying to make her change her mind about marrying him. He wasn't being fair. He had told her he wouldn't be possessive but if he wouldn't see her again unless she agreed to marry him he was being possessive.

At times she was unbearably lonely without him for he made her feel so precious to him and she felt she couldn't stand another day without seeing him. At other times she was determined not to forgive him for treating her like this. They had a business to keep going and things to discuss. Just supposing he decided he no longer wanted to be her business partner, either. Then all the pleasure would go out of her work. Collecting works of art, selling them, writing about them, had always been a great joy to her and Nicholas had added to that. It had been wonderful to work with someone who appreciated the same things. They had been so in tune with each other.

It was Wednesday evening and she hadn't seen him since Sunday night. She decided to make herself a drink and a sandwich and have an early night.

And then Nicholas came.

She heard the door bell and when she saw him standing there all her anger disappeared.

"Nicholas!"

"I couldn't stay away any longer," he said.

She was in his arms before he even entered. "Oh, my love," she murmured, and then they were kissing and laughing and kissing again.

"You have been hateful," she said, drawing him in, "leaving me for so long. You can't love me as you say you do."

"I know I'm hateful," he agreed. "I wanted to punish you for not wanting to be my wife. But now I don't care so long as I'm part of your life. I can't do without you. This is proof. You've been on my mind all the time."

When they could tear themselves apart he looked at her drink and sandwich and said, "Can you spare some for me?"

"Of course I can. I would have prepared something special if I'd known you were coming. How long has it been since you had a good meal?"

"I haven't been hungry for food," he said, giving her a cheeky smile.

But he was hungry now and soon scoffed all before him, and she was happy to watch him. "I was thinking of having an early night," she said.

"Want me to spend it with you?"

"What do you think?"

They finished supper, left the dishes where they were and drifted towards the bedroom. She felt him pull down the zip of her dress and she stepped out of it and then she was in his arms. "Three days without love to make up for," he whispered, and she knew he was really going to make up for it.

In his arms all resentment, anger and frustration melted away for both of them. They loved and talked and loved again until the night was almost over and then they slept late into the morning.

They lingered over breakfast which was prepared for them by Kate's daily woman who never gave any signs of being shocked to know that Nicholas had spent the night with Kate. In fact she didn't blame Kate at all for allowing such a fine handsome man to share her bed. Like Sharon, she envied her.

Now Kate and Nicholas were ready to discuss business and Nicholas told her he hadn't been lazy over the past few days. He had been notified by someone in the trade that there was to be an auction at a country mansion not far out of London. Some pieces were to be sold privately. The house had belonged to an old couple who had lived a lifetime there. They had allowed the house to deteriorate, not realising that the contents had increased in value and were worth so much they could have sold just a few of them to keep the place well maintained. Their son, who had settled abroad, had returned to get everything settled up now that they were gone.

So that was where he'd got that coffee pot dated seventeen thirty five which was engraved with armorials within a rococo cartouche of foiliage and shells, and the Victoria cups and goblets. Nicholas had picked up some real bargains and was happy and so was the son, having received far more from Nicholas for the goods than he had anticipated.

"We shall make a thousand or two on that deal," said Kate.

She was able to tell him that she'd contacted Mrs Blackham and was fairly certain of selling a lot of Lord

Marston's antiques to her. "She just has to get the go-ahead from her husband, she says, and I think she pretty well gets all her own way."

"Don't all women?" he smiled.

"No," she retorted. "If I'd had my way over the past few days I'd have had you shot for completely ignoring me."

"You bloodthirsty little devil," he laughed, grabbing her, and kissing her savagely to make her pay for that comment.

As they drove to the gallery they discussed their forthcoming holiday in the Loire Valley. Nicholas was letting his hand wander up Kate's thigh as she was talking, "Happy?" he asked.

"I should feel happier if you would keep your mind on your driving," she smirked.

As soon as she saw them together Sharon could tell they had made up their quarrel or whatever it was that had kept them apart and made them so miserable. There was always a radiance about them when they were together.

Sharon gave Nicholas a smile. It was lovely to see that happy look on his face. If he were her young man she would want to keep him looking happy like that always.

"Have you got your passport, Sharon?" he asked. "We shall be on our way to France in a couple of weeks time."

"No, I haven't," she said, looking a little alarmed, and Nicholas assured her that there was no need to panic. "Come along. I'll take you right away to get one."

"Oh, what about my hair?" she said, putting her hand to her head. "I can't have my photograph taken like this."

Kate laughed. "Don't you know that passport photographs always look frightful anyway? Go along with Nicholas, he knows where they take passport photographs."

There was a photographer within walking distance and Sharon felt quite small walking beside Nicholas, though she wasn't short.

"You look tired. Had a busy time

this week?" he asked, as they waited for the photographs to be developed.

"Quite good. But even if you are not selling, people ask a lot of questions demanding your attention. At one time I had dificulty in answering their questions, but I'm learning about antiques all the time."

"I've been in the business for years and I don't know all the answers," he said. "Fortunately we usually know more than our clients which makes them think we are smarter than we really are. You'll be an expert yourself one of these days, Sharon."

They had a good laugh over her passport photograph. He said. "You don't look quite as bad as that," teasing her.

"I sincerely hope not," she giggled.

He put his arms across her shoulders in a companionable sort of way as they walked back to the gallery, telling her that they would be going to France by air. "We can hire a car while we're there, or the Louviers might allow us to use one of theirs."

"How long will we be staying?" asked Sharon, when they were talking about the holiday with Kate.

"About three weeks," said Kate. "It will take that long to get all the information I require, but it will take much longer to write a book, of course. We shan't be working all the time. We all need a holiday."

That evening Sharon decided to pay a visit to her parents in order to tell them about the wonderful holiday she was going to have in France. She knew they'd be pleased for her.

There was no travelling in a luxurious car to her parent's home. She had to catch a bus out of the city and another to get to the housing estate where they lived. The house was a modern semi-detached, nicely furnished, with a welcoming atmosphere.

Before her father's accident there had been a car in the drive and they had enjoyed a good standard of living. Their life style seemed more realistic to Sharon than the life style of those in the minority who lived in stately homes, or mansions, or a manor.

Nevertheless it had been an enjoyable experience for her to visit Kate's home and she could tell her mum and dad all about it. It infuriated her to see her father in a wheel chair for he was not very old and had always been full of life. It was distressing for his wife and daughter to see him like this and they were praying it would not be for always.

They were delighted to hear that Sharon was going to the Loire Valley. "But won't it cost a lot?" asked her mother.

"No. Kate said it won't cost me a penny."

"She's very good to you. She must value you."

"I should hate to have to work for anyone else now. She and Nicholas are fine to work with."

She stayed with her parents quite

late, hoping she'd cheered them up a little. They were very proud of her. "She's almost as beautiful as you were at her age," said her father to her mother when she left.

4

Here

IT was evening and Sharon was actually walking with Kate and Nicholas in Paris — Ville Lumiere — The City of Light. Public buildings, churches and monuments were floodlit, making this beautiful city look even more impressive than during the daytime.

Even Kate and Nicholas were enjoying the spectacle and they were used to travelling and seeing delightful places. They had walked for hours mingling with the tourists and Sharon had loved every minute of it.

The last two weeks in England seemed to have fled to Sharon. She had been excited, yet terrified, at the thought of flying and it had been Nicholas who had calmed her nerves, telling her to relax and enjoy it. "It's great, really," he told her.

He had actually held her hand as the plane rushed through the air and became airborne and then he'd made her look down below to watch the landscape become like a giant map. The coastline appeared in no time and they could see the ferry boats on the channel like miniatures.

Sharon thought Kate might resent the attention Nicholas was giving her but she seemed amused by it. She was used to travelling and had no nerves.

The affair of Kate and Nicholas was having ups and downs. There had been days during the past fortnight when they had been idealistically happy, but other days when Nicholas had not seemed so.

It was Kate who was making Nicholas miserable. He had hoped when she had accepted him back so enthusiastically after his absence of a few days that she would change her mind about marriage, and he took her to see a beautiful house in Surrey which was for sale. He longed for a house in the country where he could live with his wife and family, rather than live in a flat in London. Kate had declared that it was a beautiful house but had not given him any reason to believe she would be prepared to live there with him.

Kate didn't seem to be aware of what she was doing to him. He couldn't love her more and she was obviously in love with him. Why was she so reluctant to give herself to Nicholas in marriage? He was perfect in Sharon's eyes and she kept asking herself this question. She couldn't bear to see him unhappy over Kate.

But tonight both he and Kate seemed on top of the world. They had taken Sharon to see as much as possible. At the end of the Bois de Boulogne that afternoon they had caught a bus to the Bagatelle, Jardin and Roseraie and had tea in the beautiful garden restaurant.

They were staying at a smart hotel in Paris overnight and Paul Louvier had arranged to pick them up tomorrow to take them to their beautiful chateau.

It wouldn't have surprised Sharon if Nicholas had booked one room for himself and Kate, but he hadn't. They had their own rooms, but Sharon saw him leaving Kate's room the next morning when she was venturing a look out of her own and he gave her a look which seemed to say he knew what interpretation she would put on that.

"Sleep well?" he asked.

"It was rather noisy," she smiled.

"I didn't notice," he said, and took her hand as they went downstairs.

He always looked so happy when Kate was being nice to him. "Kate won't be down yet," he said. "Care to come for a walk?"

"I'd love to," she said.

"This is le boulevard Haussmann, famous for les grands magasins," he said, and went on to tell her that Haussmann was responsible for the construction of the sewer system which ran beneath them.

"If you were with your boy friend

I'll bet he'd want to take you down there. You can take a trip through the sewers in little boats and electric powered trucks."

She screwed her nose in disgust. "He would have to go on his own," she retorted.

"Have you a boy friend?" he asked.

"I haven't met one yet that I would like to go with seriously."

"And then you would like to get married?"

"Oh, yes," she said, emphatically.

"I wish Kate felt that way," he said, solemnly. "It's she who is dodging the question of marriage, not me."

"And yet she was very unhappy when you didn't see her."

"Strange, isn't it?" he said.

"Yes. She needs you."

"She puzzles me. I don't think she can understand herself at times."

"Perhaps if Kate thought there was a danger of losing you to someone else, that you could transfer your love to another, she could consider marriage."

"You think I should try and make her jealous?"

"I'm sure she'd hate to see someone else taking her place."

"I'd like to put that to the test."

"You would have to explain to the girl you chose that it was simply to make Kate jealous because she could easily fall in love with you, Nicholas."

He laughed. "You're very good for my ego, Sharon. You think it would be easy to fall in love with me?"

She knew it would. "You wouldn't want to hurt anyone."

"No, I wouldn't. The trouble is I've dropped all my girl friends since I've known Kate. There's you, of course."

"Oh, I wouldn't do," she said, in alarm. "Kate would never be jealous of me."

"Why not? You're very beautiful, especially this morning. You look fresh and natural."

They walked on in silence for a time and then he said, "How would you like to pretend that we are getting fond of each other? Let Kate catch us stealing a kiss now and then?"

"Oh, no!" cried Sharon. He would know right away that his kisses were having a terrific effect on her. "You must find someone else."

"Come on, be a sport, Sharon."

"Kate's good to me. I couldn't allow her to think I was encouraging you."

"I would make it obvious that I was doing all the running."

"You could lose Kate."

"You mean she wouldn't fight to keep me?"

"Oh, I didn't say that. If she has lots of pride she would perhaps rather let you go than admit she was jealous over someone else. Particularly a girl like me."

"Why a girl like you?"

"Well, you know. I'm just nobody in comparison with a girl like Kate."

He laughed. "You think she's marvellous too? But you do yourself an injustice, Sharon. You are a very attractive young lady."

She was confused and he said, "I mean that. I think it would be a good idea to let Kate think she has competition. Let's give it a try?"

"I think we've already made a start," she said, glancing at her watch. "We've been out a long time and she must be wondering where we are."

"You're right," he said, but he didn't hurry. Instead he caught her in his arms and gave her a breathtaking kiss. She felt her heart start to flutter and the colour rushed to her face. "There," he said, "that's given you a colour. Now we'll go in hand in hand smiling happily."

She went to snatch her hand away he caught it firmly, and then she tried to treat it all as a joke as they entered the dining room, but she knew there was guilt written all over her.

If Kate noticed they were hand in hand she didn't comment. "You are an energetic pair," she smiled. "Where have you been?"

Sharon had known all along she

wouldn't be jealous of her very ordinary secretary.

Nicholas let go her hand as if reluctantly and went to sit beside Kate. "I've ordered breakfast," she said, "you must be hungry."

The waiter came along with fresh coffee and assured them that their breakfast would not be long. Kate said she'd ordered English breakfast and Nicholas said that was good. "I like bacon and eggs when on a holiday. Do you, Sharon?"

She agreed that she did.

Kate was wearing a white dress with spaghetti type shoulder straps revealing her lovely shoulders. Her hair looked simply glorious, so rich and dark. Sharon had to keep looking at her, and she had that effect on Nicholas too.

Her lovely soft brown eyes rested on Sharon, fondly. "You are looking more relaxed already, Sharon. You were ready for a holiday."

"I can't believe this is really me," said Sharon.

"We shall have to make you a more important member of our business," said Nicholas, "and, then you'll be able to afford to come abroad more often."

"Yes, I agree," said Kate. "I heard you telling a client all about a piece of porcelain she admired and it was your salesmanship that sold it. In a year or two you'll be as knowledgeable as we are."

"You deserve a raise in salary," said Nicholas, and Sharon went hot. Was this part of his plot to make Kate jealous? Was he trying to make it look as if he appreciated her more than he did in reality?

After breakfast it was agreed that they'd go for a walk on the banks of the Seine before Paul arrived. They weren't expecting him until later.

"It's a pity you haven't a young man with you, Sharon," said Kate, and Sharon immediately coloured up, feeling that Kate had noticed after all that Nicholas was being rather more attentive towards her than necessary. It made her feel uncomfortable.

"A boy friend would get tired of hanging around while I was working," said Sharon.

"I hardly think so," said Kate. "There must be lots of boys who'd be only too pleased to hang around for you."

They enjoyed their walk along the Seine, Kate and Nicholas naturally interested in les bouqinistes, antique dealers who sold their wares from wooden boxes along the quai walls. They watched the bird dealers and seed dealers in the old houses, all very different from anything one sees in England.

They had a fine view of the 'Notre Dame' quarter from the east with the massive silhouette of the cathedral, but they had to return to the hotel for they didn't want to keep Paul waiting.

When he arrived he was accompanied by Yvonne who said she didn't intend to miss the lovely run through the valley. "The car is large enough to seat three in the back," she said.

Paul Louvier was looking marvellous in cream suit and shirt, a perfect partner for his beautiful wife dressed in a lemon summer dress. "I wonder if she has to diet to keep so slim," Kate whispered to Sharon.

They dined before setting off with Paul and Yvonne and over the meal they discussed the high quality wines produced in the Loire Valley. "The vineyards extend nearly to the sea," said Paul. "There are many producers, ranging from the large firms at Saumur and Vouvrey to small concerns operating on almost a cottage industry scale. But if I start on the subject of wines I shall never stop."

"You will be able to tour all round the Loire Valley," said Yvonne, "and you'll learn a lot about the different wines and wine making."

"And I hope you girls have brought your bikinis," smiled Paul. "We must get some sunbathing in too."

"I'll bet you'll look great in a

bikini, Sharon," said Nicholas, and she supposed he was again trying to make Kate feel he was taking too much interest in her. But it didn't seem to have any effect on Kate at all. He had in fact been showing far more interest in Sharon than usual all morning, pointing out things of interest to her, and yet Kate had shown no displeasure at all.

"We enjoy visitors," said Paul. "We like to show off our lovely home. We are inclined to stay at home too much, not making the effort to go far, and if we didn't have visitors we should lose touch with the outside world."

"Yes, it was a great effort to pack and make a trip to England," said Yvonne.

"Well what could be better than having your own vineyards to look after, a home set in beautiful surroundings, and a lovely wife." said Nicholas, smiling at Yvonne.

"We're very lucky," said Paul. "I often think that heaven couldn't be better than our life here."

Paul and Yvonne were like many French couples. They had decided not to have a family. There had been two bitter wars fought on French soil and they were determined not to bring children into the world to experience a third.

"Come, we mustn't linger," said Paul. "We have a good journey before us, and we want to see some places of interest on the way."

5

NICHOLAS travelled in the front of the car with Paul and the three ladies were in the back. It was large, luxurious car, so they travelled in comfort.

Yvonne pointed out all the places of interest as they went on their way through Versailles to Rambouillet enjoying the extensive wooded area so well loved as a holiday resort by the Parisians. She was a mine of information and could tell them lots about historical buildings and stories attached to them.

On the plateau above the steep banks of the Loire they were enthralled by scenery around Chateaudon. To Sharon it was out of this world, there couldn't be anything better in heaven itself. Indeed they all seemed spellbound, although all except Sharon had been this way before and there were exclamations of pleasure as the scenery unfolded before them.

"The Loire Valley is famous for its chateaux," said Paul to Sharon, "Coaches run regularly, bringing tourists to see all this splendour. We could have travelled through the Foret d'Orleans. There are a succession of simply gorgeous chateaux. At Sully-sur-Loire is a dream of a medieval castle behind a wide moat. It has parapets, drawbridge and towers with pepper-pot roofs. You can imagine Jeanne d'arc, or Joan of Arc as you call her, riding out in fourteen thirty on her last expedition."

Sharon could imagine it very well and was delighted to hear all the stories Paul and Yvonne had to tell. She had never met such charming people in her life and felt very privileged to be included in this little party.

Although they'd had a good meal at the hotel before leaving Paris they were all hungry again by the time they reached Tours. Paul said he knew a good restaurant here and they were glad when he parked the car and they were able to get out and stretch their legs. The restaurant seemed a shabby old place, but the food was excellent and they understood why Paul had chosen to come here.

"You enjoy our cuisine, yes?" asked Yvonne.

"Oh, yes, I'm enjoying everything about my trip to France," said Sharon.

"You must try some of our delicacies."

With such tempting food placed before them it was difficult not to over-eat, and Sharon noticed that Kate and Yvonne were very careful to have small portions. So they didn't keep their splendid figures without having to consider their intake of food. As usual the meal took up a great deal of time for the French do not like to rush meals.

They caught a glimpse of beautiful fifteenth century houses, some even twelfth century, wooden ones in some cases, and magnificent parks and gardens. But there was no time to linger, so reluctantly they left Tours and their next stop was Angers, another beautiful city. Paul wanted them to see the castle with its seventeen massive round towers and deep moat. "We often come into Angers for the wine exhibitions," said Yvonne.

"And we come to see the horse racing, too," said Paul. "They call Angers the 'city of flowers', it's a pity we haven't more time to spare to look around."

When they came at last to the chateau of the Louviers the light was fading but the outline of the chateau was clearly visible. The symmetry of its facades and economy in its roofline showed French classicism rather than Renaissance style.

There were terraced gardens, and the scent of flowers filled the evening air, and lime tree avenues separated the gardens from an orchard running up the hill. Groves of trees and winding paths formed a landscaped garden, which they couldn't see too clearly at this time. They were told that there were caves quite near, suitable for mushroom growing, and that they would be able to visit them before their holiday ended.

The Louviers owned acres and acres of land where they grew the finest Cabernet-Pineau d'Aunis grapes which made excellent red wine.

The homeliness of the chateau was apparent as soon as they entered. In spite of the lateness of the hour they were greeted charmingly by an elderly lady dressed completely in black. Her face was wrinkled and old but she seemed to have lots of energy and soon called upon members of the staff to attend to the comfort of Monsieur and Madame Louvier and their three guests. Rooms had been prepared for them and they followed a maid up the wide staircase and along the gallery to them.

A manservant appeared to bring their

luggage. Sharon, not used to being waited on, would have struggled with hers but Nicholas took her case and put it with the others.

Kate and Nicholas were given bedrooms adjoining each other and Nicholas gave Kate a special look which expressed satisfaction at being so close to her. Sharon was a little further along the corridor in a room no less splendid than theirs.

It would be easy to get lost in a place like this, thought Sharon, until one got used to it. Innumerable paintings illustrated historical events. There were rich decorations in marble, bronze and gold. The ceilings were all elaborately painted and there was fine panelling with ornamentation which gave an idea of the magnificence which surrounded the wealthy of bygone days.

Kate came along to see if Sharon was happy with her room and they both expressed their delight at the beautiful rooms they were to occupy and wondered about the famous people who had slept in them in the past.

"We shall learn a lot when I start writing the history of the chateau," said Kate. "I'm eager to get started."

A light meal was awaiting them in the petite salle à manger. Nicholas joined them in the corridor and they went down together.

"It's a splendid home," said Nicholas. "I feel I've stepped back in time. I can understand your fascination for the place, Kate."

They were served with Poulet Bearnaise which was absolutely delicious and with which they drank a dry white wine. This was followed by variety of fine cheeses and coffee. It had been a tiring day with all the travelling so they were ready to retire soon after their meal. They could talk tomorrow.

When Sharon entered her room she saw that her case had been emptied and her clothes were hanging in the massive wardrobes. Her nightdress was laid out on the bed for her. She was glad it was pretty and quite new.

Kate was whispering to Nicholas on the landing, telling him he couldn't share her bed while they were staying here. "If we were married the question of where I slept wouldn't arise," he said, angrily.

"But we're not," she said.

"No, I can't see that we ever will be. You don't want me, Kate."

"Please don't let's quarrel this time of night, or rather morning. Can't you see I'm tired?"

Of course he knew Kate was too tired for making love but there was pleasure in just sleeping together. It filled him with joy just to know she was close by his side. But this was a right often denied to him, although she professed to love him. He marched off without kissing her goodnight and Kate went into her room knowing that she wasn't being fair to him.

But she didn't want him tonight. There were lots of nights when she didn't want him and that was why she was afraid to marry him. She didn't want to lose him but she knew she deserved to. She couldn't get off to sleep although it was late, and told herself she should have let him stay. He would have soothed her to sleep.

She used make-up the next morning to disguise the fact that she'd had an almost sleepless night although she had been so tired when she went to bed. No one would have guessed it for she looked as beautiful as ever. She was wearing a floral strapless dress with a black background and looked really striking, as always. She went to give Nicholas a kiss, but although he didn't turn away, he was noticeably cool and Sharon knew, she could always tell, that Kate hadn't allowed him to love her last night. There was always this atmosphere of tension between them when all was not well.

Why were they behaving like this towards each other, on holiday too? It was always Nicholas who was most affected. There was no sparkle in him and Sharon wished she had the right to comfort him. She didn't believe the Louviers noticed anything amiss. They didn't know the couple as well as Sharon did.

After breakfast the Louviers took their guests on a conducted tour of the chateau and afterwards they went outside to inspect the glorious gardens which it had been too dark to see properly when they arrived. There were ponds and fountains, flowering shrubs, gorgeous rhododendrons in various shades, little streams, statuettes and bronze figures.

Kate moved to Nicholas's side and took his arm, but before long he released himself and Sharon felt most embarrassed when she discovered him at her side instead. He began to talk to her, making it look as if he preferred her company, and she couldn't help worrying over what Kate was thinking.

Kate knew that Nicholas had snubbed her in front of their host and hostess and had turned to Sharon to show his displeasure with her. She was quite aware that he was trying to make her jealous, but she was concerned for Sharon. Sharon meant a lot to her and she was vulnerable. Nicholas shouldn't use her to invoke jealousy.

She felt anger more than anything else towards Nicholas because he was simply using Sharon which wasn't fair. The looks of adoration Sharon gave Nicholas quite unconsciously had not been lost upon Kate in the past and she wouldn't want her to get hurt. Never for one moment did Kate believe Nicholas would really turn to someone else. She was certain of his love.

At the moment she was determined to get on with the work she had come to do and told Paul the sooner she started the happier she would be, so he and Yvonne took her into their study to let her see the documents and so forth which they had already looked out for her.

"I'll just go and tell Nicholas I shall be busy for the next hour or so," said Kate, and found him and Sharon wandering down a narrow little path on one of the garden terraces below. As she approached them she thought how handsome Nicholas looked in his white slacks and apricot coloured shirt. Sharon was looking particularly charming too in a white button-through dress covered with black polka dots. It was calf length and the skirt flared at the waist. Nicholas reached out to take Sharon's hand and Kate smiled. He was being so obvious.

"Nicholas!" she called. "I'm going to be busy for the next few hours."

"Very well," he said, in an offhand manner.

Sharon tried to draw her hand free. "Shall I come, Kate?" she asked. "You might want me to take some notes."

"If I do I'll give you a call," said Kate, and left them to become engrossed in the work she'd come to do.

Sharon turned to Nicholas with a troubled look in her eyes. "Nicholas,

I do wish you'd stop this game. I can't look Kate in the eyes. I feel dreadful."

"Why should you? Kate saw that it was I who took your hand in mine. She doesn't possess me, you know."

They moved slowly back towards one of the little ponds and Nicholas was still holding her hand as they watched the fountain. "What would you think of a man who allowed himself to be treated as Kate treats me?" he asked, softly. "I'm expected to wait for her call. It's like having favours bestowed on you when the donor feels inclined."

Sharon knew that Nicholas was feeling bitter because he loved Kate so much. He couldn't be blamed for showing her that he could find his pleasure elsewhere, but she didn't want him to make it look as if he were transferring his affection to their secretary. Her eyes settled on a beautiful butterfly which had settled amongst the glorious blossoms. "Look, isn't that lovely?" she said, trying to distract his attention.

"Not as lovely as you, Sharon. What have you done to yourself? You look beautiful."

She gave him a smile and said, "Don't be silly, Kate isn't here at the moment so you are wasting your time."

"I don't need Kate's presence to make me want to kiss you," he said, and to her dismay, she felt her soft slender body being drawn close to his strong hard chest. She could feel the heat from his body, and the beating of his heart as he kept her close to him for a moment, and then he bent to give her a kiss. She had wondered, when she had seen him kissing Kate, how it would affect her to be kissed in the same way, and now she knew. She could have fainted away in his arms.

When he released her she looked up at him with misty eyes and he gave her a tender smile. "You got carried away," he said. "Don't say you haven't been kissed before."

"Don't be silly," she said. Of course she'd been kissed before, but never felt shattered by a kiss as she did now.

She saw Paul Louvier approaching and said she would have to go.

The Louvier's library was massive and contained a valuable collection of leather bound books in almost perfect condition. The chateau had belonged to various people, all aristocratic of course, and their family histories were all contained in these books together with records of famous people who had stayed here in the past.

There was a catalogue listing all the treasures in the chateau which was also of great interest to Kate. She had hoped Nicholas would help her write about these treasures, but from his attitude today she feared he was going to be difficult. That was the trouble with Nicholas, she thought. He got easily hurt and it made him moody.

She supposed the Louviers would have noticed his behaviour and it made her angry with him. They might get the impression that something at the chateau had upset him. It would certainly seem strange to them to see that her male companion seemed to have transferred his attentions to the girl she had brought along as a secretary. It really was too bad of Nicholas to put her in such an awkward position. She could hardly explain that Nicholas was behaving in this way simply because she had not allowed him to sleep with her the previous evening.

Paul spent a long time with her discussing the documents available and showing her illustrations of the various rooms and treasures which would look good in a book. Then he left her alone to decide where she would begin and what information she felt was of most importance. There was enough material to write a dozen books or more.

By lunch time she had worked really well and was finding the work was beginning to take shape. She was ready to dictate the opening paragraphs to Sharon this afternoon. Once she got started she felt she would get on like a house on fire. The story was all here, it was only a matter of sifting through for the most spicy or interesting events.

She was surprised that Nicholas hadn't once come along to enquire how she was getting on. He had agreed to help her and should have got over his ill humour by now. She went in search of him.

Neither he nor Sharon were anywhere to be seen and that vexed her even more. Sharon had said she wouldn't be far away if required. It was very rarely that Sharon annoyed her. In fact she couldn't remember a single instant when she had felt mad with her, but now she felt irritable at not being able to find either of them.

She went to her room to freshen up before going down for a meal, which she expected to be announced any minute, and afterwards decided to check if Sharon was in her room. She found her lying on the bed and said, anxiously, "Sharon! Are you all right?"

Sharon shot up immediately. "Yes. Have you been looking for me?"

"I did wonder where you'd got off to. I've been looking for you and Nicholas."

"Nicholas went off in the car somewhere with Paul," said Sharon, wondering if Kate could see that feeling of guilt in her eyes because she'd enjoyed Nicholas's kiss so much. "He told me to tell you he wouldn't be long if you enquired."

She didn't tell Kate that Nicholas had tried to persuade her to accompany him and Paul and that she had refused, mainly because she had wanted to be alone to savour once again the joy and pleasure his kiss had given her.

"I expect they'll be back for something to eat," said Kate. "Lunch will be served soon."

Kate went off to her room feeling

a little put out. Where had Paul and Nicholas gone? It wouldn't have hurt Nicholas to let her know he was going out and to ask if she wanted to go with him. She wouldn't have gone because she was so interested in what she was doing, but it was customary for Nicholas to give her a little kiss when he was going off like that.

To Sharon it had been a relief when Paul invited Nicholas to go with him, and yet how wonderful it would have been if she could have stayed with him, if she had the right to be held in his arms as he had held and kissed like that again. He had asked Kate to marry him and she hadn't agreed so that it would be her own fault if she lost him to someone else. Not that Nicholas would choose Sharon to replace Kate, and even if he did, she couldn't be the one to hurt her.

Nicholas said he wanted to make Kate jealous, but she had been nowhere near when he had taken Sharon in his arms and kissed her. He had been amusing himself and Sharon hated being used like that.

Now she had to go downstairs and meet Nicholas again. How could she look at him without feeling confused? She studied herself in the mirror before going down, for hadn't he told her she looked beautiful? It wasn't meant to be taken seriously, she was sure. It surprised her that Nicholas could use flattery and flirt with a girl just to amuse himself.

Sharon felt that Kate was angry when they went down together and if that was so Nicholas had achieved his object. If she hadn't shown anger about his neglect it would have shown that she didn't care about him at all. Sharon felt she ought to explain to Kate that Nicholas didn't mean anything when he ignored her and made it appear that he wanted Sharon instead. But if she'd done that she'd have been letting Nicholas down. She was trying to help the man she loved to distraction win the girl that he loved to distraction.

It was most disturbing to think of herself walking hand in hand with Nicholas through the terraced gardens. She had been getting the kind of thrills she had no right to get for she knew quite well that he belonged to Kate. But how could she help the way her body reacted to his touch? It had seemed as if electric currents passed between them and the tingling in her hand had been so strong she felt sure he must have felt it too. Did he have no conscience? If he knew how he was affecting her it was time he stopped playing games with her. But when he had seen Kate approaching he had held her hand even more so that she couldn't draw it away.

Nicholas and Paul were late coming into the dining room for lunch and when they did arrive Sharon found the attention of Nicholas drawn to her rather than to Kate. She met his eyes and felt that perhaps he was thinking he had gone a little too far that morning, for there was something like concern for her in his expression.

She turned away and when next she looked at Nicholas he was talking to Kate and it seemed to her that he was being his normal charming self to her. The bitterness he had been displaying to Sharon seemed to have died away and he and Kate were talking together as if there had been no stress between them. He was asking her how the work was coming on and Kate was enthusiastic about it. Paul and Yvonne were adding some humorous stories of their own in connection with the chateau and Sharon tried to join in the general laughter.

When Nicholas looked at Sharon now there was no special look in his eyes. Perhaps he was regretting that he had neglected Kate that morning to play around with her. The kiss he had given her was not important to him. He had seemed amused when he had seen how it affected her and said, "don't say you haven't been kissed before," which showed that it had meant absolutely nothing to him. Well, a kiss wasn't anything these days. Not unless you allowed it to be important to you. She must stop thinking about it and forget that little episode had ever happened.

6

SHARON couldn't believe they'd been at the chateau for a whole week. They were living in the type of world she had read about but never really thought existed in these days. Everything at the chateau was perfectly organised. Meals appeared as if by magic, everywhere was spick and span yet servants never seemed to be in evidence. Visitors arrived, were entertained and stayed for meals and everything ran like clockwork.

Most mornings Kate worked non-stop and of course Sharon worked with her. She typed and retyped, for Kate was a perfectionist making alterations to improve the text all the time. But she wasn't a slave driver and when she felt Sharon had done enough she would suggest they called a halt and went out for a break. It was to be a working holiday after all.

They were near the coast and took trips to various beaches where they swam and sunbathed and had picnic lunches. Paul and Yvonne liked to come with them for they said they didn't bother to go to the coast unless with friends. Sharon would have expected Nicholas and Kate to go off their own at times, but they didn't.

La Baule was one of their favourite beaches and is considered one of the loveliest in France. There was a casina, a promenade with hotels and villas and plenty of holiday makers with entertainments for them. There were over a hundred tennis courts, there were golf courses, plenty of sailing, regattas and horse racing.

One day Sharon stayed behind on the beach while Kate and Nicholas with Paul and Yvonne went to play tennis. "I don't mind," she assured them. "I can't play tennis."

Nicholas very thoughtfully went and purchased an English paperback for her to read while they were away, and as she was reading, letting the sun make her tanned body even more so, she was startled by a terrific slam from a beach ball. She shot up, wondering at first what happened to her.

It seemed she was immediately surrounded by four young men looking very contrite. "I say, I'm awfully sorry." said one of them. "That must have hurt you."

"It did," she admitted, and then seeing they were really sorry she smiled. "I think I'll survive."

"All on your own?" asked another.

"For a short time," she said. "My friends have gone to play tennis but I can't play."

"Well come and play beach ball with us."

She looked at them uncertainly and one of them said, "Come on, it will do you good. Get some of that fat off you."

"Cheek!" she smirked, knowing she didn't carry surplus fat.

She allowed herself to be drawn into their game but after a time she was so hot she declared that she was going into the sea to cool down. It was a mistake. "We'll all come!" they cried, and chased her down to the sea. Soon she was being ducked, splashed, and all the things young men do to girls in the sea. A non-swimmer would have been mad to enter the sea with them, but she thoroughly enjoyed the fun.

She wouldn't have believed an afternoon could go so quickly. "I must go," she cried, "my friends will be waiting for me."

And indeed Nicholas was right there watching their carryings on. "Have you been back long?" she asked.

"No," he said, studying her carefully. She was wearing a blue bikini and she saw he was regarding her from top to toe though he'd seen her in it before. "It didn't take you long to find company," he said. "Four young men, weren't there?"

She looked at him in surprise. He

sounded critical. "They were nice boys. English. We've been having fun."

"I could see that. You'd better hurry, we're going for something to eat."

"I'm sorry if I've put you out," she said, stiffly.

"Oh, that's all right," he said. "But you'd better hurry and tidy yourself up."

She could see that he wasn't in a very good humour and supposed that he and Kate were not the best of friends yet, but there was no need to have it out on her. He made her feel like a little child who had been misbehaving.

"Sorry if I've kept you all waiting," she said, when they reached the others.

They assured her that they didn't mind and were glad to see her having so much fun. But for all that she hurried to make herself presentable in order to go with them for something to eat.

They sat on the forecourt of a café and Sharon, rather subdued, listened to the others talking without joining in the conversation.

"You're quiet," said Paul, who liked to tease her a little, as Nicholas did. "Are you all right, Sharon?"

"Yes," she said.

"She's furious because I dragged her away from her boy friends," said Nicholas.

"I am not!" she snapped, and the others laughed at this show of temper from Sharon for it was most unusual.

"I expect you're feeling odd one out on this holiday," said Kate.

"Oh, no, you've all been very kind to me," said Sharon. "This is the best holiday I've ever had in my life."

They noticed as they were driving homewards that storm clouds were forming. They had been extremely lucky with the weather so far, it had been beautiful. Indeed the sun had been shining so much there was danger of forest fires and everyone was saying that rain was needed.

Terrific peals of thunder could be

heard and before they had reached the chateau the rain was coming down so fast the windscreen wipers couldn't cope and Paul had to pull up in a lay-by until the rain ceased to fall so heavily. The lighting was so vivid it seemed to come right into the car where they were sitting.

"I can't believe I was sunbathing such a short time ago and there wasn't a cloud in the sky," said Sharon.

"And it was so hot when we were playing tennis," said Paul. "This rain will clear the air."

They watched it form into streams and then rivers as it rushed down the road. One or two claps of thunder were really ominous, seeming immediately over their heads. But after a time the lightning was not so vivid though the rain came in torrents.

At last it ceased and before long they could see steam rising from the roofs and roads as the sun came out again. Everywhere looked clean and fresh and the countryside much greener.

That night Sharon lay in bed thinking about the book Kate was writing. Mistresses of famous dukes had lived here at the chateau and Sharon imagined the dukes to be like Nicholas and the ladies like Kate. From the portraits of the ladies she could picture them in their beautiful gowns looking absolutely splendid and being thoroughly spoilt by their lovers.

She remembered the way Nicholas had spoken to her on the beach, making her feel a little cheap. "Four young men, weren't there?" It was nothing to do with him if she'd attracted every man on the beach. In her dreams he appeared to her in the sort of dress worn by dukes years ago. But he wasn't being very nice to her. Of course, she wasn't Kate.

When she went down to breakfast she found herself glancing at Nicholas all the time, seeing him as she had seen him in her dreams. He seemed aware of her observation for each time she looked at him he was looking at her.

Later Sharon joined Kate in the study. "I wouldn't mind writing full time," said Kate, "but there isn't the money to be made writing as there is in dealing with antiques."

"I thought writers made a lot of money?"

"Only if they write best sellers."

"So you couldn't afford to become a full time writer?"

"I could, I suppose, but I wouldn't have the standard of living I have now unless I lived with my parents."

Through the window they saw Nicholas talking to Paul and then they both got into Paul's car and off they went. "He hasn't been a great help to us, has he?" said Kate.

"Perhaps he feels superfluous," said Sharon. "You do seem to be able to cope without him."

She saw Kate look at her rather strangely and found herself colouring. Did Kate think she meant that she was able to cope without him all the time? They were not particularly close this holiday. Friendly, but no signs of great love between them.

Working together, Sharon and Kate had got on very well and Kate discovered that Sharon had a knack of presenting phrases better than she did herself. She would apologise for expressing something better and Kate told her not to do that. "I appreciate what you're doing and it seems to me that you should be the one to take up writing, not me."

Yvonne announced that she and Paul were giving a dinner dance at the end of the week and had invited a number of friends. "I'm sure you'll enjoy it," she said. "We arranged to have it while you're here so that our friends can meet you, and it will be something else for you to remember."

"Did you bring an evening gown, Sharon?" asked Kate, when they were alone.

"I did but I don't know whether it will be grand enough."

"Well you've worn some very nice

clothes so far. You have good taste."

"Thanks," said Sharon, thinking that she might have even better taste if she had the money to spend on clothes that Kate did.

She showed her evening gown to Kate. It was of classical design, nothing fussy, in a soft silk, sea green. Sharon slipped it on and Kate nodded approval. "That's lovely. Suits your colouring very well. If you get your hair done in a sophisticated style you'll look as good as anyone."

Later Kate told Nicholas she would like to do some shopping. She asked Sharon if she would like to go too, but Sharon thought it time that Kate and Nicholas got off on their own in order to get back on their normal footing. She watched them go and returned to the study to get on with the typing of the fascinating book about the chateau, soon finding herself lost in the historical events. Kate was putting over the atmosphere of the chateau very well and Sharon was sure the book would read better than a book of fiction.

When she'd finished she sat thinking about Nicholas and Kate. She wanted them to be on good terms so must not be depressed at the thought of them being out together. But he filled her thoughts all the time. He had been so nice to her. She tried to persuade herself that it was only a crush she had on him such as girls had on television stars, film stars, and so on, but the trouble was that Nicholas was not out of reach as they were. He had walked with her, held her hand, kissed her, paid her compliments, looked into her eyes intimately when Kate was around, all to make her jealous, and all the time he had been causing her to fall deeper in love with him. She had to admit she did love him. Had done for a long time, but had known it was hopeless.

The atmosphere was getting oppressive again and Sharon felt sleepy so she retired to her room and lay on the bed. She hadn't intended to stay long but fell into a deep sleep. When she awoke she realised it must be almost time for their evening meal. She had time for a shower and changed into a strawberry pink dress. It was the first time she had worn it and catching glimpses of herself in the long mirrors as she walked along the corridors she could see that she didn't look too bad.

She couldn't see anyone around and went out into the gardens. Turning a corner she came upon Nicholas stretched out on a garden lounger with his hands clasped on his chest and apparently asleep. She sat in a nearby chair and watched him. He looked very comfortable; it would be a shame to have to wake him for dinner.

A wasp came buzzing round and Sharon hated wasps. She kept perfectly still hoping it would go away, but it was being very persistent and she waved her hands about to send it away. It hovered over Nicholas and she was afraid it might sting him so she went carefully over and tried to waft it away from him. Several times she flapped her handkerchief at it and then suddenly a hand shot out and grabbed her, drawing her down and she found herself being thoroughly kissed. Nicholas hadn't been asleep after all and had obviously thought it was Kate moving near him trying to get rid of the wasp.

"H'm" he murmured, his eyes still closed, "I've been wanting to do that."

Then he opened his eyes and found himself looking straight into the eyes of Sharon. "I'm sorry," she said. "You thought I was Kate. I was trying not to wake you, but a wasp was buzzing round you. I was trying to send it away."

There was laughter in those deep blue eyes as they met hers and she wondered if he had known all the time it was her and not Kate. He was a terrible tease, and he was still hanging on to her hand when they heard footsteps approaching.

She snatched her hand away and

turning saw that it was Kate. She must have thought it was most unusual to see Sharon leaning over Nicholas in that fashion and in confusion Sharon said, "Nicholas mistook you for me, Kate. I thought he was asleep and was trying to shoo a wasp away which was hovering over him. I didn't want it to sting him."

The words came rushing out; she had to keep talking to hide her confusion.

Nicholas met Kate's eyes and they looked at each other for a long time. Sharon felt that Kate didn't believe for one moment that Nicholas had made a mistake and, hoping Kate didn't think she had been making herself cheap leaning over a man like that, she fled indoors.

Something told her that Nicholas had known it was not Kate all the time so why had he kissed her like that? He knew the effect his kisses had on her for hadn't she nearly swooned in his arms the last time he held her close and drew the breath from her body?

Perhaps he had known that Kate was nearby and had made another attempt to try and make her jealous. If that was so that little trip out together on their own had not been satisfactory after all, for if it had been Nicholas would not still be wanting to make her think he was taking a fancy to Sharon.

Sharon would have gone back to her room but Yvonne met her in the hall. "Just in time, Sharon," she said, with that charming smile of hers. "Dinner is just about to be served."

She waited by the windows as if she were interested in something going on outside, but for once she was not seeing the beautiful gardens, the fountains and gorgeous blossoms. She was wondering what Nicholas had said to Kate when they were alone, or whether Kate had taken him to task for kissing Sharon. Perhaps Kate wouldn't say a word because she was not the type to show jealousy, and she wouldn't give Nicholas the satisfaction of knowing whether she cared or not if he kissed

Sharon by accident or design.

When they came in eventually Kate looked directly into Sharon's eyes as if she wanted to say something, and Sharon felt the hot colour rush to her face. That annoyed her, for she had done nothing to feel ashamed about, but that tell-tale colour would make her appear guilty, and Kate had found her bending right over Nicholas.

If Kate had any sense she would let Nicholas know that she was ready to marry him whenever he wished and then he would behave himself, Sharon was sure of that.

7

KATE had been surprised to see Sharon hanging over Nicholas but she felt sure she hadn't been forward enough to go and make advances to Nicholas. She said he had thought she was Kate and she had no doubt that he had told her that, but she doubted whether he had really mistaken Sharon for herself, even in a half asleep state.

She knew that Nicholas was almost certainly missing their love making. Over a week now since they'd slept together. She knew she hadn't been fair to him, allowing him the privileges of a married man and then withdrawing them when it suited her.

When Sharon had left them Nicholas had looked at her with a look of defiance which had been almost a challenge for her to say something about his behaviour, but she knew she hadn't the right of a wife to express disapproval of his behaviour. She didn't intend to act the role of a jealous female, but she worried about Sharon. Nicholas had a magnetic personality and she could imagine the effect he could have on a young girl. He had taken possession of Kate who had given up all interest in other men since she'd met him.

She knew that Nicholas was probably trying to bring her to her senses and agree to marry him and if they'd been alone in her flat she would have been prepared to talk seriously about it. Since they had been here she had often wished Nicholas would insist on sharing her room occasionally, but he had made no advances at all, sometimes forgetting to wish her goodnight.

"It's time for lunch," she had said, calmly, and he rose slowly to his feet. When they entered the dining room Kate was perfectly charming to Sharon and there was no awkward atmosphere between the three of them, though it had not escaped Kate's notice that Sharon had looked guilty and confused, and a little upset.

As for Nicholas himself, he was asking himself why he hadn't gone out of his way to try and make Kate change her mind. He had been sure on occasions that she would have welcomed him into her arms, and in the past he would have jumped at the chance to take her, so what was holding him back now? He was aware that people are not always in the mood for love and made allowances for Kate when she didn't want him, but had always been grateful to her when she did. But now he felt himself putting a barrier between them. He'd gone off with Paul whenever he had the opportunity which would never have happened back in England. He had only wanted to be with Kate.

He supposed their work would bring them close again but he had wanted marriage and for Kate to want it too. If she accepted him now would it be just because she didn't intend to let him get away from her? Or because she wanted marriage as much as he did?

He felt thoroughly fed up and became cool towards Kate and Sharon, and Sharon felt that something had been said about her behaviour. It worried her.

But plans were going ahead for the dinner dance. Yvonne was busy helping with arrangements, Kate took Sharon off on the day of the event to get her hair dressed, and Sharon felt like brushing it all out when she left the salon.

The hairdresser had gone into raptures over her hair, telling her how the sun had bleached it and how he would make her look like a princess. Sharon wished she could have left her hair in its usual style.

"You don't make the best of yourself, Sharon," said Kate. "There will be some very important people at the chateau tonight and who knows? You could win yourself a wealthy husband. You are quite lovely you know."

All this was embarrassing to Sharon, who didn't want to win a wealthy husband. She just wanted to be herself. But she knew Kate meant well and left her hair as the hairdresser had dressed it, high upon her head. It wasn't her at all.

When they returned to the chateau Sharon stayed in her room out of sight feeling too self-conscious to meet anyone, especially Nicholas, she was sure he'd laugh at her.

Kate dressed beautifully for the occasion. She was wearing a pure white evening gown with sparkling jewels. The gown hung in beautiful folds and was in striking contrast with her dark hair. Sharon knew that her own dress looked nothing in comparison with Kate's.

Sharon had always believed that being well dressed and having a sophisticated hair-do would give a girl all the confidence in the world but instead, as she went down with Kate, she knew she had never felt so self-conscious in her life. She would have given anything to stay in her room.

Nicholas came forward to speak to them looking terrifically handsome in his well cut evening suit. His glance went from one to the other and he told them they both looked very charming.

Sharon was taken into dinner by a nephew of Paul and Yvonne. He was in his early twenties and a very polite young man, eager to please. His name was Jules Louvier and Sharon wondered if he would have exerted his charm quite so much if he had known she was an ordinary working girl and this was the first time she had ever appeared at a grand occasion like this.

Seated at the table Sharon looked round at all the women with their elaborate hairdos, wearing expensive jewellery and fine clothes, and the men looked so formal their evening suits that she told herself they were a funny lot. Dressing up to look like peacocks.

The table was set with elaborate cutlery, fine dishes and tableware. Extra staff had been employed to wait on them and everything was absolutely splendid. Jules was talking to Sharon and she suddenly wondered what he would think if he saw her as she often appeared in London wearing jeans and a jumper, dashing down to the corner shop to get herself some fish and chips to save cooking just for one.

The thought was so amusing to her she felt she was going to have a fit of the giggles. She pressed her hand to her mouth to stop herself laughing out loud and it was then that she saw Nicholas's eyes resting on her across the table.

It was almost as if he knew what she was thinking. He saw the amusement in her eyes and was laughing as he turned to thank the waiter who was serving him with delicious sea food.

Jules wondered what he had said

to make his companion's eyes dance with merriment. He thought she was wonderful and Sharon need have no fear of being left out of things when dinner was over.

He remained by her side and danced with her over and over again. Sharon saw Kate looking into the eyes of Nicholas in that intimate way she had and Sharon did her best to give all her attention to Jules. She had even got so far as asking Jules to let her try out her schoolgirl French on him and they were having lots of fun over the blunders she was making, but she had been dying to try out the language ever since she arrived in France.

When Nicholas came to ask her to dance she felt her heart leap with fear and joy. She wouldn't be able to keep in step with him as Kate did she was quite sure, but it would be marvellous to dance with him.

He was a good dancer and she found she could follow his steps once she got used to his style. He was so tall he seemed to tower over her. She couldn't think of a word to say and they danced quite seriously for a time and then he said, "what was so funny at the dinner table? What had young Jules Louvier said to amuse you so much?"

"It wasn't he who amused me," she smiled.

"No?"

"It was just that I suddenly felt such an idiot sitting there dressed up like a dog's dinner."

He laughed loudly at her expression. "You look very charming. A real lady."

"It's not me at all," she grinned, and put her hand up to touch her hair to see if it was still in place.

"Whose idea was that? Kate's?"

"Not really. It was the hairdresser. I think he enjoyed himself seeing how high he could make it."

"I'd like to have a go at doing your hair myself," he laughed. "Would you let me?"

"How would you do it?"

"Oh, I'd let it fall round your face

down to your shoulders."

The thought of Nicholas doing her hair sent little shivers through her and he said, "what was that for? Not cold, are you?"

"No," she said, feeling that nothing escaped him.

"Jules Louvier hasn't taken his eyes off you since you were introduced. What do you do to men? Hypnotise them?"

"What do you mean?" she asked.

"Oh, you know. What about the other afternoon. We left you for an hour or so and return to find the young men flocking round you."

"You think I make myself cheap?" she asked, indignantly.

"I didn't say that. I'm just commenting on how easy it is for you to get male attention. You give the men a look from those big blue eyes and draw them towards you."

"Deliberately? You mean I go out of my way to attract a man's attention?"

"Don't you?"

"No, I don't."

"Is there someone in your life you would like to attract towards you?" he asked.

"Yes," she said, and wondered what he would say if she said she was having his attention at the moment, and that he was taunting her, trying to make her angry.

"Did he mind your coming away for three whole weeks?"

"No," she said. "He couldn't care less about me. In fact he's in love with someone else."

"I don't believe you. A man couldn't be in love with someone else if he could have you."

"You're being very flattering," she said, "but it is possible, I'm not that irresistible."

The music finished and he took her back to Jules who was waiting for her to rejoin him. "I wouldn't say you weren't," whispered Nicholas, and it wasn't until he'd gone that she realised that that was his answer to her statement that she wasn't irresistible.

"Who is that man?" asked Jules, looking none too pleased.

"Nicholas? He's my employer," said Sharon. "See the lady he's just joined? I work for them. Your aunt and uncle kindly allowed me to join this dinner party but I'm really out of my class."

But her confession seemed to make no difference to him. In fact he was still interested in her relationship with Nicholas.

"Are you in love with him?" he asked.

"You're very inquisitive," she smiled. "Why do you ask that, anyway?"

"Well you were quite pink when you came back to me and I just wondered."

"Nicholas is not for me," she said. "He's in love with that beautiful girl he's talking to."

When the party was breaking up Jules asked Sharon for her London address. "I'd like to come and see you when I come to England."

Some of the guests were staying overnight, including a German couple, Frieda and Konrad Ehlers, who spoke English very well but with a different accent to Paul and Yvonne. They were friendly with Kate and Nicholas for Yvonne had made a special point of introducing them and telling them the work Kate was doing while she was here.

At breakfast the topic came up again and Paul explained that Kate and Nicholas were experts on antiques. Kate had helped them catalogue quite a few of their treasures some time ago, some of which had been hidden in cellars and so forth during the war.

"Many of our treasures were lost during the war," said Konrad. "It was a wicked shame that so many beautiful works of art were lost or destroyed."

"But it's surprising the number that were taken away and hidden for safety," said Frieda. "Lots of them keep coming to light. People who hid treasures were often killed and no one knew where to find valuable pictures, silverware and so on. It must be wonderful when people suddenly discover a hoard of treasures."

Konrad turned to Nicholas. "I have been thinking of having an up-to-date catalogue drawn up of the art treasures in the schloss. It's a beautiful place and escaped great damage during the war. My father took great care to see that beautiful paintings, porcelain and other works of art were taken to a place of safety. We use only a part of the schloss for our living accommodation. The rest is on view to the public, and I'm sure the value of many of the items must have increased tremendously since the war."

"Probably much more than you imagine," said Nicholas. "Items valued at a few hundred pounds twenty or thirty years ago are valued in the thousands today."

Konrad was thoughtful. He turned to his wife, "Frieda, I think we should have our catalogue updated. And this is your type of work, Nicholas and Kate? Would you like to take the job on? We could let you have a few works of art cheaply in part payment for the work."

"Well, we never refuse work," said Nicholas.

"Just let us have a rough estimate of your charges and we'll fix a date for you to come. You could make a holiday of it, as you have done with Paul and Yvonne."

Sharon couldn't help thinking how easily things come to some people. Just as one stay at a glorious chateau had come to an end they were being invited to stay in a German castle.

When the Ehlers left they were quite confident that Nicholas and Kate would be taking on their work for them and they extended the invitation to include Sharon too. "I suppose you will need your charming assistant," said Konrad, giving Sharon a very friendly smile.

Kate and Nicholas agreed that they relied upon her a great deal, Nicholas giving Sharon a wink which seemed to be telling her that another free holiday was on the agenda for her.

With the departure of the guests came the arrival of another and that was Jules Louvier. He said he'd come to thank tante Yvonne for the lovely dinner party but he didn't fool anyone. He'd come to see Sharon again.

It was pleasing to know he'd come to see her. She didn't feel odd one out now.

"You should have stayed the night," said his aunt, who was obviously very fond of him.

He grinned. "You didn't ask me to."

Yvonne spread out her hands expressively as the French do. "Since when have you needed to be asked, Jules?"

Today he was dressed quite casually in blue jeans and yellow tee shirt. He looked quite different from the young man who had been elegantly dressed last night for the dinner party.

Perhaps he had gone home to get out of his evening suit into something more casual.

It was not long before he invited Sharon to go for a walk in the garden with him, and he flashed her a smile showing even white teeth.

As soon as they were alone he said, "Glad to see me?"

"Of course I am," she said.

"I wish I'd known you were here before, I'd have been over days ago."

It was not long before Nicholas joined them and suggested that Jules and Sharon might like to join him and Kate in a run to the coast for swimming.

"Oh, yes, fine," said Jules, looking to see if Sharon liked the idea.

He had his swimming trunks in the car, he said, and suggested they all went with him in his sports car.

When Nicholas returned to tell Kate they were going out with Jules and Sharon she said, "Was that your idea? I suppose it didn't occur to you that as

Jules has come specially to see Sharon he might not want our company?"

"They've only just met," he said. "They can't have got to the stage where he wants to be alone with her already."

"How do you know?" asked Kate. "I do believe you don't want Jules to go with Sharon."

"We're responsible for Sharon."

"Oh, goodness, Nicholas, he's Yvonne's nephew. He wouldn't get up to tricks with one of her guests and she wouldn't encourage him to be friendly with Sharon if he wasn't to be trusted. Anyone would think you were Sharon's guardian."

"I still think we ought to keep an eye on them."

"Yes, grandpa," smiled Kate. "I'm sure Sharon is perfectly capable of looking after herself but if Jules has agreed to our going I suppose it will be nice."

Jules put his foot down on the accelerator and they arrived at the coast in no time. The breeze blew at Kate's and Sharon's hair in the open sports but by this time Sharon had combed out her elaborate hair-do and her hair was nearly to her shoulders again. Jules had touched the ends of it when they were in the garden and told her she looked even prettier than she'd done last night.

Full of energy, Jules had hardly got to the beach before he got Sharon to join him in the sea. It was beautifully warm and Jules swam with strong, swift strokes but Sharon could keep up with him.

Later they were joined by Nicholas and Kate. Sharon shrieked as Nicholas came towards her, his intention obviously to pull her under. He knew she could take it for hadn't he watched those fellows doing the same the other afternoon?

"I'm keeping away from you two," laughed Kate when she saw them both lifting Sharon out of the water to throw her back in again. But Sharon was enjoying every minute of it.

She lay on her back and kicked her legs, covering them with spray, knowing she was asking for trouble and she screamed to Kate to come and help her when it came.

Kate swam away from them. She had no intention of being ducked.

In the water Jules looked like a young schoolboy in comparison with Nicholas. He was years younger, of course, but it seemed more obvious when they were in the sea. Nicholas had stronger shoulders and a good hairy chest. When he laughed she saw his strong white teeth and watched the drops of sea water trickling down his brown body in fascination.

The sea had flattened his hair to his head but it had gone into ringlets whereas Jules' had gone straight and lank. It was unfair to make such comparisons for Jules was a very nice young man, but she couldn't help it.

Nicholas came swimming towards her and as he got nearer she dived right down beneath him and popped the other side of him.

"You wretch," he shouted, "I'll get you."

But Sharon was an excellent swimmer and it wasn't easy for him to catch up with her.

"Let's swim out to that rock," she suggested. But Kate judged the distance and told them to count her out. "You go, Nicholas," she said, "I'm going out now."

And so the three of them swam out to the rock and climbed on to it. They sat there panting, the sea dripping down their backs. After a short rest Nicholas said he couldn't leave Kate on her own and made a neat dive into the sea to swim ashore to her. Jules watched Sharon as she watched Nicholas swimming strongly to shore.

"And now I've got you on my own," said Jules, when she turned her attention back to him. "You're great fun. I'm glad Nicholas suggested we came swimming, aren't you?"

"Yes, I love swimming. It's one thing I do well."

"One amongst many others," he smiled. "You dance well too. I'd like to discover more about you, but your time is running out, isn't it?"

They sat talking on the rock for quite a time before returning to the shore. They swam back leisurely. Sharon was in no hurry to see Nicholas and Kate lying side by side on their beach towels looking into each other's eyes as she was sure they must be doing now they were alone.

But Nicholas was smoothing sun tan lotion on Kate and then put some on himself. "Watch your fair skin doesn't burn, Sharon," he said, and would have put some on her back for her but Jules beat him to it.

Then Sharon had to oblige Jules. She couldn't help comparing his lean back with Nicholas's broad one. It gave her no thrill at all to spread the lotion over him, but she was sure she would have enjoyed rubbing it on for Nicholas who was watching her keenly as she performed the job.

They had plenty of time so they spread out the towels to lie in the sun doing absolutely nothing. As they lay there in their brief swimming outfits Kate slid her hand into the hand of Nicholas and Sharon saw his fingers close over hers. It filled her with pain, though she cared so much about them both.

She turned to look at Jules and pretended that she was completely fascinated by him. He was very nice, anyway.

That was all the encouragement he needed. As she turned on to her stomach he did the same and his arm stole across her back. She wouldn't hurt him for the world, but she longed to fling his arm aside. The only one she wanted to put his arm across her was Nicholas and he was lying there hand in hand with Kate.

8

KATE could feel the anger coming from Nicholas through her finger tips as he held on to her there on the sands. There was no tender pressure from them. She turned and met his eyes and saw anger in his eyes too. She had often seen him moody, perhaps a little sulky, but had never seen such cold anger in his expression as she saw now.

"Nicholas!" she said, in a soft pleading voice that the other two couldn't hear.

His fingers didn't relax their hold. She felt he would really like to hurt her. He continued to give her a cold hard glare. She knew it was a long time since they'd made love and he missed it the same as she did, but need he look so savage?

She pulled his hands up to her

mouth and let her lips press against it but it didn't soften him. She had chosen the wrong time to try and make things right between them. How could he respond here on the sands surrounded by people?

He turned away, closed his eyes and pretended to be asleep, not before he had noticed that Jules was holding Sharon's hand as they lay side by side with eyes closed, letting the sun bless them.

Kate seemed the only one who couldn't relax for a time. She was thinking seriously now about herself and Nicholas. She often treated him casually but she didn't want to lose him and it seemed she might if she wasn't careful. She had been too sure of Nicholas, she was afraid.

That evening Nicholas slept with Kate. He knew she wanted him without her having to invite him into her room and so he just went in with her. But she felt he wasn't at all loving. She lay beside him and said, "you are still angry with me?"

"Well?" he said.

"What does that mean? Well?"

"Well why shouldn't I be angry with you? You just use me for your sexual satisfaction, Kate, nothing more."

"You know that isn't true," she whispered, with tears in her eyes. "You are the most important person in my life."

"When you want me. When I've satisfied your sexual desires you can manage without me until you need me again."

"Nicholas! How can you say that? You know it isn't true."

"Do I? There are men like that. They are all over a woman when they want sex but when they've had it they can forget her until they want her for that reason again."

"Nicholas! You know I'm not like that. You know I need you. I would lose all interest in the business if I didn't have you to work with me and it makes me unhappy when I know you are."

"Kate, you don't love me! Not as I love you."

"I have never wanted anyone else since I've known you."

"When you love someone you want to be with them all the time, not just at bedtime when it suits you."

"You're being disgusting. Making me feel awful. I don't want you just to satisfy me." But even as she said this she was asking herself if that were true. Was that all she wanted Nicholas for. No, no, it wasn't, she told herself. She loved him. "Things will be different when we get back to England."

"Things would have been all right here if you hadn't shut me out of your room. What am I? I can't claim to be your husband; you're not even my common law wife because we don't live together."

"You're unusual, you know. It's usually a woman who clamours for marriage."

"I'm not *clamouring* for marriage," he said. "I'm just telling you that if

127

you loved me you would want me all the time, not just when you feel you can put up with me. And I'm not talking about sex now. Often you don't want me."

She smiled and stroked his face, gently. "So I suppose I'll have to marry you."

"You don't *have* to. You have a choice."

"We'll talk about it when we get back home."

"Putting me off again?"

"No. We'll talk about it. Make plans. Now will you love me again, properly? Not in anger as you did before."

He didn't turn to her joyfully as she expected. He lay without saying a word and she knew he didn't believe that she would seriously make wedding plans when they went back. Did she believe she would herself? She didn't want to lose him, but did she want to marry him? She began to wonder if she was normal. Most women would have given anything in the world to have a man like Nicholas for a husband. Yet something always held her back.

She put her hand on his chest and slowly moved it down towards his stomach. Usually it took no more than that to arouse him, but he lay perfectly still. Then with a deep sigh he turned towards her and took her again, but she still didn't feel that sense of satisfaction that he normally gave her. What was wrong? Had she hurt him once to often?

Sleep did not come to her quickly as it usually did after they'd been making love. She lay awake for a long time and knew that Nicholas was awake too. Usually they talked and held each other until they went to sleep. She felt very sad, as if something beautiful had ended.

The next morning Sharon saw Nicholas leave Kate's room. He did not greet her with a happy smile as he had often done in the past when he knew that she knew what he'd been up to. Instead she thought he looked rather annoyed, as if he was not at all pleased to be seen coming from Kate's room.

But he began to spend more time with Kate in the study, helping her a great deal to get all her facts sorted out and looking up important details for her. The three of them worked hard for the days were flying as they always do towards the end of a holiday and Kate wanted everything cut and dried while she was here to talk to Paul and Yvonne on the subject. Sharon was kept typing and retyping while Kate or Nicholas added a bit here or took out a little there.

Once or twice Jules called to take Sharon out. She wished he wouldn't while they were so busy but when she declared that she had work to do Kate told her not to be silly. "You can finish off the typing when we get back home if Nicholas and I make sure we have all the details we require."

It was nice to go out with Jules but it worried Sharon when he hinted that he had fallen in love with her. She couldn't honestly say that she felt anything like that happening to her. He was very nice and she enjoyed his company, but that was different from being in love.

He encouraged her to speak in his own language and she was learning all the time. "You'll be speaking it like a native with a little more practise," he said.

Again he told her he would come and see her in England and Sharon hoped it was just like the promises people made on a holiday and never kept. She wouldn't want him to think a lot of her for nothing.

He took her to town and round the shops with the intention of buying something for her but she steered him away from the expensive jewellery shops. She didn't want to feel under any obligation to him, which she would if he bought her an expensive gift. In the end he bought her some Yves Saint Laurent perfume which was expensive enough.

Yvonne was quite amused to see the attention her nephew was paying Sharon and did nothing to discourage it.

And then it was time to leave France. Their three weeks had ended and there was business to attend to back home. Kate declared that she would have to give them a ring if she found she had missed some vital points when she came to complete the book.

Jules came to see Sharon on the last day and took her out into the garden to give her a goodbye kiss. Perhaps if she saw him regularly she would fall in love with him, but she didn't really expect to see him again. Holiday romances rarely come to anything.

But he pleaded. "Don't forget me, Sharon."

"I won't," she assured him.

She was on her way to her room to collect the last of her bits and pieces and was conscious that Nicholas was behind her. "You've been very generous with your kisses," he said.

"Does Jules carry you away? Make you all dreamy-eyed and unsteady on your feet?"

He knew he had that effect on her himself and she knew he was making fun of her. "Have you been spying?" she asked.

"Of course I have," he said. "I've been intrigued. After all the kisses he has given you do you think I would still have the power to thrill you?"

"You're not going to have the chance to try," she said, laughing, and began to hurry in front of him, but he increased his pace too. "You can't catch me," she said, stupidly, as she ran forward, for it was a challenge he couldn't ignore. In a couple of strides he had her in his grip. He was laughing and she would have screamed out if they hadn't been in someone else's place.

She struggled on until she reached her room and intended to rush in and shut the door but he prevented that.

Before she knew where he was in the room with her.

"In your bedroom," he said, giving her a teasing look. "Am I the first man to come to you in your room?"

"Stop it," she laughed. "What would Kate think if she saw you in here with me?"

"We could tell her we were only trying a little experiment. Just to see if I can thrill you as much as Jules can."

"No experiments," she said, firmly.

"No? Not just a little one?"

He caught her wrist and drew her towards him. She could have released herself because he wasn't being tough, simply holding her lightly, but she didn't resist. She couldn't have done to save her life. She wanted him to kiss her. Oh, she wanted it so much, and he did. He may have intended it to be just a playful kiss but it didn't turn out that way at all. His mouth closed over hers and she found the blood pounding in her ears as his kiss went on and on. His hands held her close, moving caressingly over her back and drawing her closer to his body. She was clinging to him, making little moaning sounds as she responded to him.

"If we were alone," he said, "you know what would happen to you, don't you?"

That brought her to her senses and she began to push him away. "Nicholas, don't do this," she pleaded.

"Are you in love with Jules?" he asked.

"That's none of your business," she said, trying to recover her full senses.

"You can't be. You haven't known him long enough. And you allow him to kiss you, so why not let me?"

"You know why."

"Do I?"

"Because you love Kate, Nicholas."

"I'm a free man."

"You wouldn't like Kate to find us like this," she said, for he still had his arms around her waist holding her close to him.

"I wonder how much it would bother

her," he said, musingly.

"We haven't time to find out," she said. "I came up here to gather the rest of my things. They'll be waiting for us, and look what you've done to me. Made me all hot and bothered."

"You didn't tell me if I thrill you as much as Jules does."

"I'm not telling you," she said, and began firmly to push him away.

"Just one more kiss," he said, "and then I'll go. Maybe I'll never have the chance to kiss you again."

She should have refused, but she didn't. In fact she lifted her face to receive it but this time it was just a pleasing kiss leaving her wishing it could have been like this first kiss, but they had to be sensible. It was time to go. He left her room saying he would be seeing her downstairs shortly and Sharon stood like someone in a dream, unable to think clearly to look around and make sure she was leaving nothing behind.

She put her hands against her face

trying to cool her cheeks before going to join the others. And as she went slowly downstairs she wondered if there would ever be another man in her life who could affect her with his kisses as Nicholas did.

All their luggage was stowed away in Paul's huge car for he and Yvonne were taking them back to Charles de Gaulle airport. Jules looked so sorrowful because they were going, Sharon allowed him an extra kiss and caught Nicholas's eyes as she drew away from him. She looked back for a last view of the chateau as they set off, Jules following in his sports. He gave a toot on his horn as he turned off and they waved to him until he was out of sight.

"Are you shedding tears?" asked Kate.

"Trying not to," she smiled. "He is rather nice."

"He thinks you more than nice," said Yvonne.

Sharon was included in the goodbye

kisses at the airport and she thanked the Louviers for the best holiday of her life.

They were back in London so soon Sharon could hardly believe it. Nicholas insisted on driving her to her parent's home first and her home looked so tiny after the gorgeous chateau. "Down to earth," she exclaimed to Nicholas as he helped her with her luggage.

Nicholas smiled at her. "Have you been in heaven?"

"I certainly have."

"Have a good rest tomorrow," called Kate. "See you at the gallery on Monday."

Sharon's mother came to the door and was introduced to Nicholas who told her he'd brought her daughter home all in one piece. He said they couldn't stop as it was so late and he had to take Kate home. Kate waved to her mother from the car.

To Sharon's surprise Nicholas gave her a kiss before he left her and she was still glowing from it long after she got indoors. Lucky Kate! Tonight he would hold her in his arms, she had no doubt, and Kate didn't appreciate him as she should.

Before Sharon began to talk she wanted to know how her father was and was thrilled to hear that he had seen a specialist who believed an operation would relieve pressure on his spine so that he could walk again. That was better news than anything Sharon had to tell them.

They talked until the early hours of the morning, even Sharon's father, and he looked much brighter than before she went away because he had been given hope of a recovery from his injuries.

Kate and Nicholas were sleeping together but Kate had an uneasy feeling that Nicholas was not the same. Even after they'd made love she couldn't rid herself of the idea that something was lacking. It kept her awake for a long time, consequently she slept late and Nicholas was preparing breakfast when she eventually got up.

She watched him as he glanced idly through the papers when they'd finished eating, and was afraid if she wasn't careful she was going to lose him so she said, "Nicholas, I promised I would discuss our future when we got back. I've been thinking things over very carefully. If you wish we will announce our engagement and fix a wedding date."

He looked at her in surprise. "I don't believe it!" he said.

"You don't look over the moon," she complained.

"Well, as I said, I can't believe it. You're quite sure?"

"Yes," she nodded, and now that she'd finally made up her mind she felt quite happy about it.

He put the paper down, uncurled from the easy chair and drew her into his arms. "And you're going to share a house with me?"

"That one in Surrey if it's still available."

"It needed some renovating."

"We could stay here until it's ready."

He drew her close and kissed her. "You'll have to forgive me for not giving whoops of joy. I can't take it in yet."

"We must let our people know so that they can announce the engagement."

"They must have been expecting us to name the day before now. When will the wedding be?"

"I thought as soon as we return from that trip to Germany to Frieda and Konrad."

"Not before?" he asked, giving her a sideways look.

"There will be arrangements for the wedding. Mother will expect a big do."

He grimaced and she laughed. "I am their only daughter, after all."

"Well perhaps it won't be so long. We may as well get that trip to Germany during the summer months so it will have to be soon. I'll get in touch with Konrad. I've thought about that house in Surrey such a lot Kate. It was beautiful. I hope it hasn't been sold."

Kate felt that Nicholas wasn't terribly excited. He would have been over the moon a few months ago at the thought of getting married. Had she spoilt everything by making him wait so long?

"I'll get in touch with the agents about the house tomorrow," he said, and Kate thought that might put him on top of the world if the house was still available. It could be. Houses weren't selling that easily these days.

They spent the day quietly talking about their business and wondering how the gallery had been doing in their absence.

"If Jules comes and takes Sharon from us we're going to miss her," said Nicholas.

"I know, and we'll be lucky to get anyone else like Sharon. Apart from her business ability and her usefulness, I'm very fond of her. I could never look on her as just an employee."

Nicholas sat thoughtfully. "She seems to have grown up and become more beautiful since she started working for us in the beginning. If she leaves us perhaps we'll give the gallery up. We don't depend on it."

"It was your idea," said Kate. "But I hate to think of Sharon leaving us and letting the gallery go."

"We shall have to cross that bridge when it comes," he said.

Sharon had already started work in the office making a note of all that had been sold and deleting them from the stock book. "How's it going, Sharon, being back at work," asked Nicholas, entering the office.

"I'm not altogether with myself," she grinned.

"Are you pining for your boy friend?"

"Jules?" she shrugged, "I don't suppose I'll see him again.

"I'm sure you will," said Kate, who had come to join them. "He didn't seem the type to say he'd come to see you if he didn't mean it."

"I'd rather he didn't," said Sharon. "Holiday romances never come to anything, do they?"

"You never know," said Kate.

"Kate and I are going to get an engagement ring," said Nicholas, looking directly into Sharon's eyes.

"Oh," said Sharon, and immediately thought of that little scene, just before they left the chateau, in her bedroom, and colour rose to her face.

"She's finally accepted me."

For a moment Sharon's eyes met his and held. "I'm glad for you, Nicholas," she said, "I'm glad for both of you. I'm sure you'll be happy."

"Thanks," he said, and Sharon turned to give Kate a kiss. Did she know how lucky she was? She had always had everything she wanted, it seemed, and now she had the most wonderful man in the world.

When Nicholas and Kate left shortly afterwards to visit the jewellers Sharon looked after them, wistfully. She wanted them to be happy. Had wanted it all along with all her heart and they were going to be so why did she feel like bursting into tears? She had known all along that Nicholas belonged to Kate.

She had helped Nicholas to make Kate jealous and it had worked. Kate would never know how much she cared for Nicholas because she hadn't witnessed all the tender little scenes there had been between her and Nicholas. The time he had kissed her by the fountain, she could almost see again that lovely butterfly that had come to rest on the nearby blossoms.

And Sharon was almost certain she'd given herself away when Nicholas had kissed her in the bedroom at the chateau. She had moaned with the pleasure of his kiss and he had held her so tenderly against him. He had made her fall more in love with him than she already was. She thought of the expression in his eyes when he had announced that he was going to get an engagement ring for Kate. Did he look like a man over the moon with joy? She had seen him on occasions look much happier.

9

THE following weeks were full of activity and the holiday in France began to seem like a dream. The engagement of Kate and Nicholas was announced and the press gave details of their family backgrounds. Sharon was surprised to learn that Nicholas was the son of a well known judge. She had never connected his name with his father and wondered why it had never cropped up in conversation that he was the son of a famous father.

Another surprise was to learn that Sir John Darcy was connected with several large industrial concerns the income from which no doubt helped a great deal in the upkeep of their stately home. She supposed that was how Kate had got to know Mrs Blackham whose husband was an industrialist too.

Wheels within wheels.

Sharon was invited to their engagement party and was introduced to the parents of Nicholas and she discovered that his father looked nothing like a judge should look, stern and rather frightening. He was handsome, like his son, and seemed full of humour.

After the party and all the excitement of the announced engagement had died down a little Nicholas began making arrangements for their visit to Germany. The Ehlers had suggested they might like to spend a few days in Eastern Germany where they had relatives. It would be an experience for them, and though Kate and Sharon didn't much care for the thought of visiting Eastern Germany he persuaded them to agree. He had discovered there was careful attention to detail and formality from the East German authorities, but he would attend to all that.

During this time Sharon's father was admitted into hospital for his operation and she was glad he was having this treatment before she left for Germany, otherwise she would have had to refuse go. She couldn't have left her mother to cope on her own. Nicholas was extremely good, running her to the orthopaedic hospital to visit her father, and he got to know her parents very well.

Travelling with Nicholas alone in his car wasn't helping her to get over her feelings for him. She knew he belonged to Kate, but she thought about him all the time, and it was no use any other male trying to win her affection.

Kate had told her that Nicholas was not going to sleep with her again until they were married.

"We are behaving like a respectable courting couple," she smiled. "He says he wants it like that so that when we marry, our honeymoon will be more exciting. We shall come fresh to each other. But I have the feeling he also believes that I might change my mind about getting married if I am sure of him without."

Nicholas shared the delight of Sharon's family when it was discovered that her father's operation was successful and that he would walk again in time and be completely cured. He hugged Sharon and her mother when the doctor told them the good news. There were tears of joy and Sharon was sure that Nicholas felt quite emotional too. No one would have believed she was nothing more than an employee to him.

Kate was kind too, taking over Sharon's work while she was at the hospital, though she left the clerical work for her to do and Sharon took it home with her to keep everything up to date.

There was also the finalising of the book about the chateau and they were all kept extremely busy. The manuscript was sent off to the publisher, Nicholas was attending to the purchase of the house in Surrey which was still on the market when he enquired; and he was making arrangements for renovations to be carried out while they were in Germany.

Sharon was taken with them one Sunday to have a look and she couldn't express her feelings when she saw it. It was in a beautiful setting, Nicholas couldn't have found anything better. Kate watched Sharon's expression as she looked around and wondered why she, too, didn't feel so enraptured. She had tried to imagine herself living here with Nicholas but no matter how hard she tried she just couldn't and there were times when she wondered if she were going to die or something because she couldn't visualise her future with Nicholas. It was a frightening feeling because it was as if something was telling her that she would never live in the house.

Nicholas was bound to notice that Sharon's enthusiasm was greater than Kate's, and she suggested all sorts of opinions about furnishing it, though it was nothing to do with her. Kate was the expert anyway, but both she and

Nicholas were interested in Sharon's ideas for colour schemes. "You shall help me furnish it when we come back from Germany," said Kate.

Nicholas came to stand beside Sharon when she was looking across the lawns and beautiful gardens. "You really are spellbound," he smiled.

"Kate doesn't know how lucky she is," she declared.

"She's always had so much," said Nicholas. "She takes everything in life so much for granted."

"Except you," said Sharon.

"Perhaps me too," he said, dryly, but turned to smile at Kate when she joined them.

A few days before they were due to leave for Germany Jules Louvier did come to see Sharon, though she hadn't expected him to. Fortunately he, arrived on a Sunday when Sharon was at her parents home. Mr Moore was back at home walking with the aid of sticks, which he was told he would be able to do without in time.

No one would have believed that Jules came from such a different background to that of Sharon's family. He was so pleased to see her again he probably didn't notice her home or anything else. When Sharon's mum said he was welcome to stay with them while he was in England he accepted the invitation gladly and lost no time in bringing his things from the car.

Sharon went with him to the guest room which was always kept spick and span and he dumped his things on the bed and then turned to her, joyously. "Sharon! Are you glad to see me?"

"Of course," she smiled, and accepted the kiss he gave her.

"I've never stopped thinking about you," he told her.

She felt rather guilty because she'd hardly given him a thought. He was just part of a very lovely holiday. She had remembered more the times when Nicholas had walked hand in hand with her in the gardens of the chateau, just to make Kate jealous, and it had done the trick.

She was happy to be able to spend the day with Jules, but told him she was a working girl and would be able to spend little time with him after today, especially as they were going to Germany very shortly.

"I'll come to your work with you," he said. "I haven't come to see London, I've come to see you and Nicholas won't mind if I stay with you in your magasin will he?"

"It won't be very exciting," she smiled.

"I shall be with you," he said, quite contented, and Sharon decided to make it a nice visit for him. After all, his aunt and uncle had made her very welcome in France.

And they spent nearly all of Sunday alone, going for a run in his car into the countryside. He had come across on the ferry from France so that he could have his car with him. He seemed very young and boyish to

Sharon because she was comparing him with Nicholas. But they had lots of fun together, especially when Sharon tried to converse in his language. It worried her when he said he wanted to marry her.

"Jules, we hardly know each other," she protested.

"We do," he insisted.

"It would change my whole way of life," she said. "I would have to come and live in France, and I'd be like a stranger there."

"How far is France away these days?" he asked. "You could come back to England as often as you wished until you were settled in my country."

"I would have to think about it a lot before I decided," she said.

"But you will think about it, Sharon. Say you will think about it."

"I'll think about it," she promised.

She didn't return to her flat while he was in England for he ran her backwards and forwards to the gallery. Kate and Nicholas were glad to see him and gave him a warm welcome. It amused them that he was willing to stay in the gallery with Sharon, and they insisted that she took some time off to spend with him.

Nicholas invited them to go to a dinner dance with him and Kate at his expense for he felt it was one way of repaying in a small way the hospitality they had received at the Louviers.

They had a lovely evening but Jules was perceptive. "I wish you liked me as much as you like Nicholas," he said.

"Oh, Jules, it's not that obvious is it?"

"It must be obvious to him too unless he's blind," said Jules.

"Nicholas belongs to Kate," she said, "and I'm very fond of both of them."

"Do you think there might be a chance for me, someday?" he asked.

"Well, if love starts with liking someone . . . "

"Yes," he said, eagerly, drawing her close to him. "That's a good start. I'll have to be patient. I shall come and see you as soon as you return from Germany."

His short stay was soon over and Sharon admitted to her mother that she did like him very much. But whether she could leave England to live in France with him was another matter.

The day drew nearer for their departure to Germany and Sharon thought it might be the best thing for her to give up her job at the gallery when they returned. The only way she could forget Nicholas was to stop seeing him everyday.

Mrs Moore didn't like the idea of her daughter going into Eastern Germany, and she told Nicholas so on that morning when he called to pick her up. "You have no need to worry," he said. "Tourists are welcome there these days. She won't land in jail or anything like that unless she does something very stupid."

Sharon's luggage was put in the car and they went on their way to pick Kate up after Sharon had wished both her parents goodbye, glad to know that her father was now walking almost normally.

"I like your old man," said Nicholas.

"Oh, goodness, you'd better not let him hear you say that. He's not much older than you are."

Nicholas flinched, and she laughed. "Dad's only in his early forties, you know, and it seemed strange to hear you call him the old man."

"Do you think I'm old?" he smiled. "I'm how many years older than you are?"

"More than ten years," she said, knowing he was past thirty. "But I don't think of you as that much older."

"I'm glad of that," he grinned, making his way through the traffic.

When they called for Kate, Sharon saw that she looked absolutely stunning. She was wearing an ivory coloured suit and brown silk blouse. At the side of Nicholas in his dark grey Savile Row suit they looked a perfect couple.

"Well, Sharon," smiled Kate, "here we go again. Are you excited?"

"I am, very, are you?"

"Yes, I'm looking forward to it. I haven't travelled in Germany a great deal. I've travelled through the country rather than stayed in it. I've seen the Black Forest with Nicholas. That's an unforgettable experience."

"Konrad is arranging to meet us at Frankfurt am Main," said Nicholas. "They live between Bonn and Mainz in the Rhine Valley."

"Is the Rhine Valley as beautiful as the Loire Valley?" asked Sharon.

"I don't know. I've been told it's very beautiful and that there are numerous castles along the banks of the river."

"Did you study Goethe's poetry at school, Sharon?" asked Nicholas.

"Some of it," she said. "He wrote Dr. Faust, didn't he? The man who made a pact with the devil."

"Dr. Johannes Faust inspired him," said Nicholas. "He was an alchemist and black magician, famed during his lifetime for his unquenchable thirst for knowledge."

"Hitler cast a spell over the Germans too," said Kate. "He seemed to have hypnotic powers, that was why so many people followed him." She looked at her watch. "We're in plenty of time, Nicholas."

The sun was shining as it had been when they set off for France earlier in the year. Everything seemed fine. They little realised that this trip to Germany was going to change the lives of all three of them.

10

THE Ehlers lived in the area known as the Rhineland-Palatinate just a little south from Koblenz which is in the heart of the middle Rhine region.

Koblenz is said to be the most romantic section of the Rhine which has cut deeply between the heights on either side. Little wine villages line the shores, and castles or ruins stand on every hill. It was in this region that the castle belonging to their German friends stood on a hill top.

The imposing building, towered and turretted, was totally surrounded by trees. Very different from the chateau in the Loire Valley but just as beautiful. Frieda gave them a warm welcome and took them to the part of the castle which was used for living accommodation. Most of the building was open to the public so that they could admire the many treasures displayed.

The Germans love straightforward, wholesome dishes with plenty of variety and there was a delicious meal waiting for them. They were to discover while they stayed with the Ehlers that Frieda was a most energetic person and very often prepared meals herself simply because she loved cooking and being domesticated.

Frieda and Konrad were both very fair, Konrad being tall and slim, much taller than Frieda who always looked immaculately dressed even when she was busy doing household chores. Her hair was a silvery blonde and her eyes a clear blue.

They lingered over meals chatting together and during these conversations Konrad told them that his father had been distantly related to the aristocratic barons to whom the castle had belonged through the centuries and he had been the remaining survivor after the war so the castle, still intact, had passed to him though he'd seldom visited it in the past.

It had been a responsibility his father had been reluctant to take on, but Konrad said he'd been delighted to keep it going when it passed to him, and it had been his idea to open the castle to the public as he felt they had as much right to share in the pleasure of these treasures as he had himself He considered himself more as a guardian of them rather than the possessor, though the entrance fees charged to the public gave them their greatest source of income.

The stories related about the people who had occupied the castle in the past were just as intriguing as the stories in connection with the chateau in France, and their visitors found it a temptation to sit listening to Frieda and Konrad instead of getting on with their work.

But they made a start, and there was a lot of work involved. In the Knight's Hall were the weapons and armour. There were rich furnishings and outstanding art treasures including collections of Roman antiques, medieval art and sculpture and paintings by many European masters. In another section of the castle was a porcelain collection, also jewels and glassware.

They could easily have been distracted from the work for from the terrace they had a most gorgeous view of the Rhine valley. It would have been much easier to take an interest in their surroundings than in the job they had come to do.

But for the first few days they concentrated almost exclusively on the task they had come to do and worked almost non-stop before accepting any invitations from the Ehlers to go sightseeing. Sharon worked hard typing out the lists for the new catalogue. Perhaps she worked hardest of them all, though of course the expert knowledge of Nicholas and Kate was most important for without their knowledge the job couldn't have been done.

And then Frieda and Konrad insisted they had a break. They had been longing to take them sightseeing and at last persuaded them to pack up working for a time to go out and enjoy themselves.

They took them on an unforgettable trip by river steamer on the Rhine. These efficiently operated river steamers make frequent stops and Frieda and Konrad made perfect guides for their guests, giving them all the historical details they could concerning the regions through which they were travelling.

They took them to see an operetta performed on an open air stage floating on the water. They took them to see buildings which had been restored after being damaged in the war. They saw scenery out of this world and when they went to bed at night could still see it when they closed their eyes, and could still hear the beautiful music.

They began to mix work and pleasure for Frieda and Konrad were so anxious for them to see as much as possible before they returned to England. They visited beautiful Heidelberg. The university there was borrowed for the 'Student Prince'. Wooded hills rise above the castle and make it look like a stage set for an operetta.

Then they would work long hours to make up for taking time off. One evening Kate declared she had a headache and left Nicholas and Sharon to carry on without her. They worked on and on making up for lost time. When at last Sharon covered her typewriter she discovered how tired she was. When she stood up she ran her fingers up the back of her neck to relieve tension and strain.

"You're very tired," said Nicholas, seeing her action. "I've worked you too hard, haven't I?"

He came to her and began to massage her neck and shoulders for her. It was so soothing she shut her eyes and gave a deep sigh.

"You like that?" he asked.

"M'mmm," she said, her eyes still closed, and she found herself being turned around and felt his mouth upon hers and that made her open her eyes in dismay. She had tried to forget those other kisses and now he was reviving her memories.

He smiled at her expression. "You deserve that for working so hard," he said, no doubt aware that he had sent her pulses racing. She could have flung herself into his arms and asked him to kiss her again, and felt that he would have done if Frieda hadn't arrived to insist that they finished work to have something to eat.

"We were just coming," said Nicholas.

He had set a longing within Sharon again which kept her awake when she went to bed in spite of her tiredness. He shouldn't have done that now Kate had promised to marry him.

There were wonderful days to follow. It was a wonder they were able to complete the work they'd come to do for they were taken out so many times. Konrad was like a walking encyclopaedia, telling numerous stories and giving them so many historical details about his country.

Sharon wished she had a companion for it was awkward being odd one out, though she couldn't complain that they neglected her. Often Nicholas would draw her to his side to see something he didn't want her to miss. But then she would see Kate holding his arm, looking up at him as they talked intimately, and it made her feel depressed. When this holiday ended she must end her association with them. She didn't know how she could explain to them that she had to leave their employ but she must.

"Are you going to do my packing for me, Kate?" asked Nicholas.

"I suppose so, you lazy thing," said Kate, giving him a smile, and to Sharon as they went to their rooms she said, "men can be so helpless."

Sharon wished she had the privilege to do things for him. She could tell that Kate was only too pleased to do the job for him. They weren't taking a lot of luggage with them.

They made an early start, flying into West Berlin from Frankfurt am Main, landing at Tegel airport. From there they caught a taxi to the exclusive Schlosshotel which was formerly a palace style residence in a quiet area. Sharon knew if she'd been paying for this holiday herself she would have had to book into a far less luxurious hotel. Kate and her companions took this sort of luxury in their stride but Sharon didn't feel she'd ever get used to such living.

After a meal they set off on a sightseeing tour. They walked down the Ku-damm avenue which was a hive of activity in the centre of the city. The Tiergarten park covers six hundred and thirty acres.

They went through zoological gardens, listened to an open air concert before going on to sample all the other forms of amusement in the vast pleasure ground.

Konrad and Nicholas climbed the Siegessaule which is a hollow column rising two hundred and ten feet high in order to see a magnificent view of Berlin. The ladies declined the offer to accompany them.

"You should have come," said Nicholas. "You can see the Garden of Eden from the top."

"The Garden of Eden?" exclaimed Kate.

They laughed and Konrad told her that there was an English Garden dedicated to Anthony Eden when he was foreign secretary of Great Britain and it is often referred to as the Garden of Eden.

They went towards the Brandenburger Tor. The Eastern sector begins a few yards in front of the Brandenburger Tor which was once the Arch of Triumph of the German capital.

They stood and looked in awe for everywhere on the East-West boundary is the concrete and barbed wire wall separating the two sectors.

Rows of houses had been bulldozed down inside the eastern sector. "That's to leave a clear field of fire," explained Konrad, making them shudder.

"If you take a walk along the Western side," said Frieda, "you can see the memorials to those who tried to escape across the frontier but didn't make it."

Sharon began to wish they were not going into the eastern sector for it filled her with dread to think about it. But Konrad had arranged to see his father's sister and her son, his cousin.

"I haven't seen them for a long time and I'd like to know how they're going on. It broke my father's heart to know that his sister was caught in the eastern sector and not allowed to leave. Her sister, Elisa, is not in the best of health or we would have arranged to bring her with us."

Konrad pointed out the entry into East Berlin which is still restricted, Friedrichstrasse, corner of Zimmerstrasse, known as 'Checkpoint Charlie.' It seemed that Frieda and Konrad would enter by another checkpoint and they would have to meet on the Unter den Linden on the other side.

Anxious to get away from the depressing wall they retraced their steps to the Ku-damm where they entered one of the sidewalk cafes with a glass lined terrace from which they could watch the activities outside.

Here they ordered delightful cakes and pastries with coffee for the ladies and the men had light snacks with beer.

They sat there for awhile and then the ladies became restless and wanted to go round the shops. The men reluctantly followed. "The shops stay open until eleven in the evening," said Frieda.

Kate asked Nicholas's opinion on gorgeous gowns. "Do you like that, Nick?" or "isn't that wonderful darling? Do you think that would suit me?" And he expressed an opinion though he was aware she would purchase what she liked herself.

They took a look round a boutique

and Sharon was looking at gowns more in her price range. She was so engrossed she didn't notice that the others had moved on. When she turned and found herself alone she didn't immediately panic. She went to the exit expecting to see them, but none of them were in sight. She stood where she was. They would surely miss her before very long.

But as minutes passed she did panic. Being alone in West Berlin, not able to speak the language, was frightening. She tried to persuade herself that it was better than being lost in East Berlin. She could come to no harm here. She would have to ask her way to the hotel if she couldn't find them.

Or could she? Wo ist-that meant where is . . . now what was the name of the hotel? She tried to remember but hadn't a clue. She'd just got into the taxi with the others.

Suddenly she espied Nicholas, on his own, looking out anxiously. She had only been there a few minutes on her own but it had been awful, she knew she was a baby, but she was so relieved when she saw Nicholas she ran forward with a cry.

Without stopping to think she cried, "Nicholas! Nicholas!"

He saw at once that she'd been really scared and he held out his arms. She ran straight into them and he could feel her shaking. He held her tight and she thought she heard him murmur, 'darling' but she wasn't sure.

"You're all right," he said, gently, as if she were a child.

"I'm all right now," she said, trying to laugh off, her stupidity. "I'm sorry I didn't see you all move away."

"We should have made sure we were all together," he said. He lifted her chin and she gave him a rather queer smile, for she was so relieved, yet almost in tears.

She found herself being held close to him and it was so nice. Then he kissed her and that was nice too. She made no attempt to release herself, just letting him kiss her again. She found herself kissing him too and tried to believe she wouldn't have done it if she hadn't been so upset. When he released her she laughed shakily.

"Nicholas, we shouldn't do this," she said.

"I know," he said. "But you did need someone to comfort you, didn't you?" he smiled.

She agreed. And there was no one better than Nicholas to do that. It seemed that he was no more in a hurry to join the others than she was. He took her hand and she laughed shakily. "I expect the others will be joining us?"

"No. I told them to stay where they were or all of us would have been running round in circles."

They put Sharon's flushed face down to the fact that she'd been worried. When she told them how sorry she was Frieda exclaimed: "No, no, we were to blame. We shouldn't have gone walking on without you."

"If you need help at any time you ask

for the British Consul," said Konrad. "Wo ist das britische Konsulat."

They went back to their hotel and Sharon wondered why she hadn't remembered the name. It was easy enough. The Schlosshotel. They went to get ready for their evening meal having discovered that there would be dancing later and the orchestra was already playing soft background music.

Sharon wore the evening dress she'd worn at the chateau. Kate looked superb in a white and gold gown, whilst Frieda wore a green dress which contrasted well with her silvery blonde hair.

When Nicholas appeared for the evening meal Sharon found it difficult to keep her eyes off him. He looked so smart and handsome and she kept reliving the joy of being in his arms.

They were served with Schlesisches Himmelreich which turned out to be roast goose with potato dumplings cooked with fried fruit in rich gravy.

"Have you got over your scare?" asked Nicholas, softly, during the meal.

"Yes, thank you," she said, blushing at the memory of rushing into his arms. He smiled as if he were remembering. He could have told the others that she had been shaking like a scared rabbit, but he didn't.

Konrad began to tell them about the relatives he was going to see. "My aunt Charlotte's father lives with her. A charming old man well into his seventies. He has a sister in West Germany and he hasn't seen her since the war ended. The last time I saw him he said he would get a permit to visit her."

"He wouldn't have any difficulty now," said Frieda. "The authorities are glad to let the older people go. It's the workers they like to hang on to."

They sat chatting until the orchestra started to play dance music and then Sharon felt odd one out again. "I'm rather tired," she said. "I think I'll go and watch television in my room."

"You won't," said Kate. "You think it's going to be awkward being on your own but Konrad and Nicholas will dance with you, won't you?" she asked, and Konrad said immediately that he wouldn't miss the chance of dancing with a nice young girl like Sharon.

When Nicholas danced with Sharon he said, "This is the gown you wore at the chateau when Jules Louvier fell in love with you."

"And I had my hair dressed up on top of my head," she smirked.

"Suits you better as it is now," he smiled.

The look in his eyes made her inside tremble. "Kate has beautiful hair," she said. "She's the most beautiful girl I know and she's always been wonderful to me."

She had to remind him that he was engaged to Kate and that she wouldn't do anything to hurt her.

She couldn't help feeling that Nicholas had changed since their stay in France.

There were times when he was serious and withdrawn. It wasn't because Kate was being anything but her wonderful self. Kate had told her that it was Nicholas who had suggested that they didn't sleep together again until they were married. Perhaps he was missing his love and that was why he was stealing kisses from another girl.

When they returned to their table Frieda and Konrad were dancing. "Aren't our German friends delightful?" said Kate. "I always thought the Germans stiff and formal, but they're not like that at all. They can't do enough for you."

"You've watched too many war films," laughed Nicholas. "The German is always shown as ruthless and cruel and I suppose in their films we are shown like that. The enemy has to be shown as such."

The following day they all went walking; because their hotel was in such a pleasing location there was no need to go far in search of beauty.

The German's passion for flowers and all forms of flora was obvious. Nearly every side street window had a box of flowers and there were splendid private gardens.

As they walked along, Nicholas and Kate were walking hand in hand and suddenly Sharon felt him take her hand too. "I'm going to hang on to you, Sharon," he said. "We mustn't lose you again."

"No, don't let go of her," smiled Kate, without the slightest sign of jealousy. Did Nicholas feel that little tingle of electricity as he held her hand, Sharon asked herself.

When the day ended they discussed their visit into East Germany the following day. "Are you feeling nervous, Sharon?" asked Kate, when they were going up to bed.

"A little," said Sharon, "but I shall be glad to be able to say I've been there."

"I keep thinking that there must have been lots of people, really nice people like Frieda and Konrad, murdered because they dared to defy authority."

"And I expect there are a lot more like them who'd love to be free."

"I'm a coward," said Kate. "I wouldn't dare to defy anyone if I thought I might lose my life."

"People must get strength from somewhere," said Sharon, "for you hear such stories of extreme bravery."

"I wonder how the guards feel when they obey orders to shoot."

"Perhaps they'd have to be brave to disobey," said Sharon.

"I believe they are rewarded if they kill someone trying to escape," said Kate.

"So they have to bribe them to be cruel."

Sharon lay awake for a long time. It would be impossible not to dwell a little on the terrible things that had taken place here, indeed in other countries too. It seemed that very few countries were completely innocent of violence at some time or other in their history.

And yet Germany was such a beautiful country. She would never forget the quaint medieval villages, with their wine tasting, the folk music, classical music, the breathtaking scenery, lakes, rivers and mountains, trips on the river, fairy tale castles, beautiful Heidelberg. So much to hold in her memory.

Even more memorable would be the looks of tenderness she had had from Nicholas. The joy of being held in his arms, and the wonderful sensation of being kissed. Could it be that he was a little in love with her? Had Kate destroyed the complete love he had had for her by making him wait her own time before agreeing to marriage? She had taken the initiative from him when she'd made him wait until she was ready to say 'yes, we'll marry.' If she had left it a little longer would Kate have lost him altogether?

Nicholas wasn't the type to play around with girls. He would never have taken liberties with Sharon in the first place if it hadn't been a game to scare Kate into agreeing to marriage. That shouldn't have been necessary. Perhaps Nicholas had found Sharon's kisses just as sweet as Kate's, she tried to persuade herself, and if Kate had gone on refusing to marry him he might have allowed something deeper to develop between himself and Sharon.

She recalled that day in the gallery when he had told her he was going to buy an engagement ring for Kate. He had looked into her eyes as if he were trying to tell her something. He had waited so long for Kate to make up her mind and now that she had it wasn't so thrilling as it might have been. But she was being fanciful. It was obvious that Nicholas and Kate belonged to each other.

She eventually went off to sleep to be awakened next morning by Kate who told her she was feeling dreadful. It was unlike Kate. Sharon never remembered her ever having much wrong with her. At the breakfast table she sat quietly, not eating, and when Nicholas asked, "What's wrong Kate?" she gave him a wan smile. "I don't know," she answered. "I have a strong feeling something is going to happen. Almost like a premonition."

"You've been allowing your imagination to run riot," he smiled, and gave her a little hug.

"There's nothing to be afraid of," said Konrad. "We wouldn't take you into danger, not for anything in the world."

Kate smiled and said she knew she was just being silly. They finished breakfast and once again their luggage was put into the hired car and Konrad waited for them to join him as he was driving them into the eastern sector.

It wasn't long before he was dropping off his English friends at 'Checkpoint Charlie' and they had arranged to meet up again on the Unter den Linden when Konrad and Frieda had passed through their checkpoint.

Konrad had booked them into the

Bercolina Interhotel and it seemed no time before he was driving them on to the car park, belonging to the hotel.

"Gosh, it's a massive place. I didn't expect anything like this," said Kate.

"We've stayed here before," said Konrad. "You will have private facilities with radio and television in your own rooms. There's a roof garden where you can get service, and there's a currency exchange shop."

They were given a warm welcome at the hotel and were to find that service was excellent. Kate was hungry, having eaten nothing since she got up, and was more then ready for the meal which was ready to be served. Burgermeister-Suppe, a delicious thick soup followed by Spanferkel, which was suckling pig and Kartoffelpuffer, potato pancakes.

"Feeling better now Kate?" asked Nicholas.

"Much," she replied. But she could have told him that she felt an air of unreality which she couldn't explain. It was as if she were waiting for

185

something to happen.

Having settled into their rooms and finding nothing at all to complain about, they went to the roof gardens to sit and relax for an hour or so. It was all very pleasing and from there they could see the newly built East Berlin. The colossal Soviet Embassy was of significant importance.

Sharon sat beside Kate and turned to her with a smile. "It's funny but I don't feel at all scared now that we're actually here."

"Neither do I," laughed Kate. "I'm looking forward to going round to see as much as possible while we're here."

Before long the men were restless. They didn't enjoy sitting doing nothing so they persuaded the ladies to get up and get ready to go sightseeing.

They found it most delightful in the Friedrichshain People's Park where the characters of Grimm's fairy tales are portrayed as fanciful fountains.

It was a nice day and crowds of

people were enjoying the beauty of the park and the fountains attracted great attention. The soothing sounds of the splashing waters were much appreciated. Sharon sat on a low wall and Nicholas came to sit beside her.

"Better than you expected?" he smiled.

"Oh, much," said Sharon. "It seems like a holiday here today."

"Well the holiday season isn't quite over," said Nicholas. "But another week or so and we shall be thinking of the autumn and the nights will start drawing in."

"It's been a lovely summer for me," said Sharon.

"For me too," he smiled. "We shall never forget this summer, shall we?"

They looked at each other and the expression in his eyes suggested that he was thinking of the same things she was. The strolls in the garden at the Louvier's chateau, stolen kisses in this country and in France, the lovely excursions they'd taken into glorious beauty spots. But most of all those little interludes when they had forgotten everyone else except themselves.

Her hand was resting on the top of the wall and she felt his fingers close over it. She couldn't think it was accidentally. If it was he could have removed his hand, but he didn't, he let it rest firmly on hers and then began to move it backwards and forwards In a caressing sort of way. She felt tears spring into her eyes. Only a few more days and then they'd be flying back to England, and then she must, she simply must get away from Nicholas. It was too painful to be near him like this, knowing that he was going to marry Kate very soon now.

She turned and found herself looking into his eyes and there was such a seriousness in them as if he too were having similar thoughts to her own. But they were joined by the others and the moment was lost.

"Why on earth do they have to

have that terrible partition?" asked Kate. "Everything would seem perfectly normal if it were not for that wall."

"Let's hope we shall see it disappear in our lifetime," said Nicholas.

"You wouldn't get me to come and live here," said Frieda.

Konrad laughed. "The Wall is said to be there to stop people from outside coming in with bad influences."

They went on their way surprised to see big stores, hotels and public buildings lining the main thoroughfares. Nicholas commented on the lack of advertising signs on the buildings which could be an eyesore as they are in many cities, and Konrad said they were probably not allowed.

They saw high rise apartments in park-like setting on the urban landscape and in order to relieve the dull and stark uniformity of appearance, coloured and ornamental panels had been put on outer walls.

"I suppose we have to hand it to them that they've raised a brilliant new city from heaps of blackened rubble and have left pleasing open spaces for the benefit of the people," said Konrad. "I believe they have thirteen theatres here including the State Opera."

"I've noticed a few bullet-pocked buildings still remaining," said Nicholas, "Perhaps they've been left as a reminder of the war."

"You could be right, they like people to remember," said Frieda.

They returned to the hotel tired and footsore after their sightseeing and after their meal were content to sit talking.

Sharon left first and decided to take a bath. Then she got into bed and turned on the radio to listen to some classical German music. Tomorrow they were going to Leipzig to meet Konrad's relations. He wanted his English friends to accompany him so that he could introduce them. "They will be glad to see someone from England," he told them.

Well, Sharon was feeling much

happier than she'd done last night. They were here in East Berlin it seemed it was going to be every bit as enjoyable as all the other places they had visited.

11

THEY set off early the next morning. Kate was looking particularly lovely in a mauve suit with white silk blouse. Her hair, thick and black, looked shiny and beautiful. Frieda looked smart too, but Sharon felt that Kate could always outshine everyone.

They arrived in Leipzig with its numerous new apartment buildings. The character of the old cities had been spoilt by bombs and these new apartment blocks had sprung up everywhere.

But Konrad's relations lived in an old merchant house which had a beautiful garden and this was a pleasant surprise for his friends who had expected to be taken to one of the apartments in the high buildings.

They were given a warm welcome

by Konrad's aunt Charlotte and her father, Herr Warneck. Charlotte was in her fifties, a rather plump, but quite beautiful person, and her father was a very pleasant man too. He had been living with Charlotte when her husband died while her son, Nils, was quite young.

In the excitement of meeting they all spoke German and were so animated the three English people could only stand and smile at their joy in seeing each other again.

And then they recovered to apologise for their bad manners in not speaking English for both Charlotte and Herr Warneck could speak English in a fashion. "You must be hungry," said Charlotte, who had received a phone call from Konrad to say they were coming, and she had prepared accordingly.

During the meal Charlotte and the old man wanted to know all about their friends and relations in Western Germany.

"Why don't you come and see

them?" said Konrad. "It would be no trouble to get a permit to come and stay with us for a holiday."

"I wish Nils were here," said his mother. "He'll be so vexed to have missed you. Why didn't you come and stay with us?"

"Not five of us," laughed Konrad. "We shall go back to our hotel tonight, but maybe we'll be able to come and see you again before we go back."

Charlotte told them about Nils. "He has a good job," she said. "He's nearly thirty. He works as an industrial chemist. Not married," she said, sadly.

He arrived earlier than he had been expected and they were all talking away so much they didn't notice him at first. He was just looking at Kate as if he couldn't believe his eyes. As if she sensed his presence she looked up and saw the tall young man with thick blond hair and blue eyes.

"Nils!" cried his mother, and then

they all looked round to see him standing there.

There was no mistaking his pleasure at meeting his relations and there were hugs and handshakes, smiles and laughter, as he was introduced to the English people. A surprising thing happened when he took Kate's hand as they were introduced. Their eyes met and it was as if time stood still. It not only stood still for him and Kate but for those looking on. It was most uncanny.

Kate felt she was meeting someone she had always known. Someone she had known throughout the centuries and it seemed he was feeling the same. They couldn't tear their eyes away from each other. Everyone waited breathlessly for them to break the silence.

"Kate Darcy," he repeated, and she felt spellbound as she looked deeply into his eyes.

Then the moment passed. He released her hand, she gave an embarrassed little laugh, Sharon had never seen Kate look confused before, and then they all began speaking at once.

They began to talk about their plans for the short time they were to be in their country.

"I've a good mind to join the party," said Nils. "I'm on holiday, did mother tell you? If I stay at home I'm likely to be on call as I've been today, but they'll have to manage without me if I'm not available. Where are you staying?"

"The Berolina Interhotel."

"I'll ring through and see if they have a room. It's busy this time of the year."

When he left the room, Kate, who had hardly taken her eyes off him since he'd arrived, went to sit beside Nicholas and she took his hand in hers. She found her hand being gripped very hard and was aware that Nicholas had noticed that she had been drawn to Nils as if by a magnet.

When Nils returned there was an air of excitement about him. "I've booked in from tomorrow," he said, and he was looking at Kate.

Time fled and later they went to the Auerbach's Keller restaurant, the sixteenth century locale of a scene in Goethe's Faust, for a meal, to save Charlotte having to prepare another for them. Kate and Nils seemed to be finding lots to talk about. She was asking him about his job and his interests. "You don't feel you want to leave this country?" she asked him.

Konrad gave her a look of warning and looked at people nearby. She supposed people were not even allowed to speak in public about trying to leave the country, or it wasn't wise to do so.

"No," said Nils, slowly. "I have never wanted to leave," and he looked at her seriously as he said it. Perhaps he was thinking now about the possibility of leaving which, of course, was out of the question.

Herr Warneck said, "Your mother and I are going to get a permit to go and see your aunt Alexandra, Nils. If I don't make the effort I'll never see her again. And your mother would like to see her sister."

"Well that's good for you," said Nils. "I wish I could come with you."

After their meal it was time for Konrad and his companions to start back for their hotel, but they continued talking, reluctant to make their departure.

"We'll come and see you again," Konrad promised Charlotte and Herr Warneck, "before we go back to our own sector."

"And we'll look forward to your visit to us," said Freida.

"It takes time to get a permit," said Charlotte, "but I'll apply immediately."

It was time for bed when the holiday group arrived back at their hotel so they went straight to their rooms.

Alone, Kate began to analyse her reaction to meeting Nils. Why had it seemed that she had known him all her life? Why did a look from him send her heart in such a turmoil? She had been stirred to the very depths of her being and something told her that he had been too. They had tried not to look at each other too much in the restaurant. He had been told that Nicholas was her fiancé and even if she'd been free he wasn't. He couldn't leave his country to spend his life with her.

How her thoughts were running on. Thinking of spending her life with a man she had just met and knew nothing about.

Her interest in Nils had not escaped Nicholas, indeed their response to each other hadn't escaped any of them, it was most strange. She had felt the hard grip of Nicholas's hand after she had been introduced to Nils and it was as if he were letting her know he was there. Her reaction had been so obvious but she couldn't have behaved differently if it had killed her.

All night she lay awake wondering what had happened to her. She kept seeing those deep grey blue eyes and wondered if he was awake thinking of her.

She was up early the next morning and slipped on a pure silk dress in pale blue. The material seemed to float around her. She had bought it for a special occasion, and this was it. She was going to meet Nils again today.

When she saw Nicholas she felt conscious-stricken when she remembered she had lain awake for hours thinking not of him, but of Nils.

"You look very beautiful," he told her.

"You won't be odd one out today, Sharon," said Frieda, as they all came together. "You can have Nils to partner you."

Kate felt a stab of jealousy which she had never felt before towards Sharon though Nicholas had often been very attentive towards her. She had caught him stealing that kiss in France, but it hadn't made her feel as she did now at the thought of Sharon being with Nils. She wanted to be with him herself and learn all she could about him.

Kate decided to get her hair shampooed and dressed. Frieda and Konrad seemed settled with newspapers so Nicholas asked Sharon if she would care to go for a walk with him.

"Did you think Nils a handsome young fellow?" he asked, as they strolled along.

"Very striking," she said.

"I'm afraid for Kate," he said. "She fell for him hook, line and sinker."

"Oh, no," cried Sharon. "She was attracted to him the same as we all were, but she's in love with you, Nicholas."

"Don't try to spare my feelings, Sharon. I'm not a fool. I could see that he was as much drawn to her as she was to him. I only wish we could go back now before Kate gets hurt."

"Kate belongs to you."

"Not yet, she doesn't. And when people fall for each other as those two did they just try to remove all obstacles. Love is a funny thing. It's stronger than they are."

"But nothing could come of an affair between them," said Sharon. "He couldn't leave here."

"That's what's worrying me," he said. "I just hope he doesn't get any foolish notions in his head. When a fellow falls in love he can be very reckless. He might even try to get through the barrier to be with Kate with tragic consequences."

"Oh, no," said Sharon, horrified.

"He wouldn't be the first," said Nicholas. "It would have been better for them not to meet again. Let's hope it's just a passing fancy. Today she might not think him so wonderful after all."

Kate entered the lounge of the hotel as Nicholas and Sharon returned. Her hair was looking out of this world.

"Very nice," said Nicholas, putting his arm around her waist. "You look beautiful."

"Thank you," she smiled, feeling

awful because she hadn't had it done for him.

Frieda and Konrad were waiting for them. "Nils not arrived yet?" asked Kate.

"No, he should be here any time. Shall we wait until he arrives?"

"Of course," said Kate, taking a seat close to them.

When Nils arrived he looked at Kate and then seemed to avoid looking at her again, and yet she could sense the pull between them. Perhaps he was remembering that she was engaged to Nicholas.

"What do you suggest we do today, Nils?" asked Konrad.

"Well it's your holiday," he said. "The surroundings of Potsdam are very nice. There are some lovely unspoiled lakes and forests more or less on the doorstep of Berlin."

They lingered over their meal talking about world events and Nils was very interested in what was taking place outside their own country. They were not encouraged to believe that the Western world was better than their own.

When they were ready to go out it was Frieda who suggested that Sharon should travel with Nils for company. It could hardly have been suggested that anyone else went with him; Sharon was a girl on her own, after all.

He accepted her presence charmingly enough and she had been watching him and Kate. They'd hardly looked at each other. Perhaps nothing happened yesterday after all. But she realised when she went through their conversation later that Nils had drawn quite a lot of information from her concerning Kate. She found herself liking him very much, he had a lovely smile showing his even white teeth, a smile that lit up his face, making his eyes twinkle.

Potsdam had a considerable industry but there were plenty of historical buildings too including the Sans-Spuci where they spent a great deal of time.

This beautiful Palace was built for Frederick the Great by Knobelsdorff. In the grounds by the beautiful pavilion Nils and Kate stood side by side and he spoke to her alone for the first time.

"It's beautiful, isn't it?" said Kate.

"Not as beautiful as you, Kate," he said, softly, making her heart beat faster. They were words she wanted to hear from him, yet couldn't believe he was actually saying them to her. She had been disappointed because he had seemed indifferent towards her today, but now she could tell that he wasn't indifferent at all.

She turned to look at him, her eyes sparkling. He smiled and said, "You brighten this place more than any other person or building could."

"Oh, Nils," she laughed.

"Oh, Kate," he mimicked. "I like to hear you say my name. Say it again."

"Nils."

"Kate."

It sounded so sweet the way he said

it. They just looked at each other, oblivious of their surroundings. And as before, the world seemed to stand still for both of them.

Sharon too watched them, and then saw Nicholas watching and her heart went out to him.

Konrad claimed Nils' attention and he walked on with him. Only Frieda and Konrad seemed unaware of the tension in the atmosphere. Kate's thoughts were in a whirl, Nils was trying to take in what his cousin was saying, Nicholas was watching Kate, anxiously, and Sharon was watching him.

Sharon knew about love at first sight, had heard about people recognising each other as if from past ages, but had put it all down to imagination of fiction writers, but now she had seen it in actual fact. Nicholas was seeing it too, and there was nothing they could do about it.

Kate would never hurt a soul and it seemed something over which she had no control, this magnetic pull towards Nils.

They went on to the outskirts of Potsdam to enjoy the surroundings, the lakes and the river Navel which flows through them. "What about going to a dance tonight?" asked Nils.

"That sounds good," said Nicholas. "Where do you suggest?"

"The café Warschau has a bar and dancing. It's on Karl-Marx Allee."

The women didn't change and the men went in their lounge suits and they set off in good spirits to the café Warschau where there was a good atmosphere and there were lots of people in festive mood.

The men provided the ladies and themselves with drinks and they all sat chatting for a while, but Nils seemed impatient to dance. He was up first and asked Sharon to dance with him. She caught a mischievous look in Nicholas's eyes as she rose to her feet, but she knew that Nils had asked her first because it wouldn't have looked right to ask Kate first. He was very tall, but a beautiful dancer, and she managed very well.

When he asked Kate to dance he swung her round to the lively music. "Were you waiting for me to dance with you?" he asked.

"Of course," she smiled.

"I mean, specially. I wanted to ask you first, but your fiancé, he might not have liked it."

"Perhaps not," she said, "and perhaps I shouldn't be dancing with you now, Nils. I'm in love with Nicholas. I wouldn't be marrying him if I weren't."

"No one can take you away from him if that's true." They danced without speaking for a time and then he said, "I could swear the same thing happened to you as it did to me when we met yesterday."

"What was that?" she asked.

"You know. It was very strange. We seemed to recognise each other, immediately. I felt you were the one I've been waiting for all my life."

She laughed, but he insisted. "Tell me you felt that way too?"

She didn't want to deny it. But there was Nicholas. He was dancing with Sharon and she met his eyes as they danced close to them. If he agreed to let her go to Nils what good would that be? She couldn't live in eastern Germany, and he couldn't leave.

"Am I being presumptuous?" he asked.

"No," she said, quickly. "It's no use denying I felt the same as you did."

"What are we going to do?" he asked. "We can't part and never see each other again."

"We have to," she said.

The music stopped and they continued to stand there. Nicholas caught Kate's arm and said, "The dance is over."

He took her arm gently and drew her away from Nils. "You look bewitched." he said, "don't let a spell be cast over you, darling, it would be disastrous."

"I know," she said, dreamily.

She danced with Nicholas but was watching Nils. The evening was almost over before he came to her again for a dance. She tried not to rise too eagerly, but her heart began to thump again as she felt herself drawn into his arms.

"I must talk to you," he said. "Can't we be alone somewhere?"

"Where could we be?" she asked.

"I'll come to your room tonight."

She looked startled and he hastened to add, "I only want to talk to you, Kate."

She loved the way he said her name but she looked at him desperately. "We must stop this nonsense. Nicholas already suspects that you have bewitched me."

"And you think it's nonsense?"

"I am behaving very foolishly. I've never acted this way before."

"And you think I have?"

"Have you?"

"No. I swear. Kate, let me come and talk to you privately in your room."

"I already lost a night's sleep last night," she said.

"There!" he said, triumphantly. "So did I. Can you call it nonsense now? We owe it to ourselves to have a little talk on our own. What harm could it do?"

"Perhaps a lot." Nicholas said it could lead to disaster.

"Please Kate," he pleaded.

They danced on and the music was approaching the finish and he said, urgently, "Please, tell me your room number."

She told him as the music finished and turned to join the others immediately.

She felt an awful traitor when she was with Nicholas for he was so attentive towards her. "You look tired," he said.

"I didn't sleep well last night," she said.

"I guessed you wouldn't. I didn't either."

"Oh, Nicholas!" she said, conscious stricken.

"You know you mean a lot to me."

"I love you too," she said.

He looked at her steadily and she repeated. "I do."

They understood each other well so there was no need for words. He wasn't a fool. He knew what was happening, but he didn't reproach her in any way. He would release her from their engagement, thought Kate. But what was she thinking? She couldn't give Nicholas up after all they'd meant to each other. She hadn't looked at another man since she'd known him, and he'd never looked at another girl. They belonged to each other.

But supposing it were possible for Nils to walk out of his country with her when she left? What then?

When they arrived back at their hotel it was almost as if Nicholas knew she could have arranged for Nils to come to her room for he lingered at her door. She felt awful for not asking him to come in, but he had kept to his vow that they wouldn't sleep together again until their honeymoon, and now she wondered if he wanted to change his mind.

"Sleep tight, darling," he said, and gave her a gentle kiss.

She didn't want him to leave her and yet it was a relief when he went. She entered her room and sat on the bed wondering how long it would be before Nils considered it safe to come to her.

There was a tap on the door and she called, 'come'.

He stood looking at her uncertainly. "I've never been in a lady's room like this before."

She offered him a chair and he sat down. "Does Nicholas come into your room?"

"Yes," she said, "and I have to tell you, Nils, that we have slept together."

"Like husband and wife. Why aren't you married?"

"Nicholas wanted to, but I have been putting him off."

"Why?"

"Not because I didn't care for him," she said, hastily. "I do. Nils care for him so much, but I didn't want to . . . " and then she remembered that she hadn't wanted to marry him because there had always been this feeling that she was waiting for someone — and it wasn't Nicholas she would marry.

"You mean something held you back?"

"Yes."

"That's how it's always been with me, don't you think that's significant?"

Of course it was. How could she deny it?

He rose and went toward her. "Can I kiss you, Kate?" he asked.

She laughed. She had wondered if he would come and try to take her by storm but he was meekly asking if he could kiss her. She lifted her face invitingly and he lifted her into his arms. It was impossible not to be carried away. It was beautiful.

He released her and he looked at her solemnly. "What are we going to do?"

"We can't do anything," she said.

"I will follow you," he said, recklessly. "I'll find a way."

She was filled with fear. "No, Nils!" she cried. "You can't. I won't let you take risks like that."

He laughed. "You won't be able to stop me, liebling. I shall come to you. You would be happy if I could be with you?"

"Don't say such things," she said. "We mustn't think about it. We hardly know each other."

"But we do," he insisted. "It hit as soon as we saw each other. We've always known each other. I have to follow you, I know it. We were destined for each other. I'm sorry about Nicholas but you would have married him before if you really cared about him."

The tears ran down her face. "But I do care about him, Nils. I love him. I can't do anything to hurt him."

"You would hurt me, rather?"

"Nils, how can we be sure that this feeling between us will last? It's

215

madness, you must see that. Just a few hours together and you're talking about risking your life to follow me."

"We can't deny how much we are drawn to each other. Fate had brought us together. I know it, just as surely as I know I've always loved you. You are mine, and I am yours. We recognised each other at once."

She wanted to hear him say these things to her. Knew she felt just as he did, but it was so impossible for anything to come of it all. And she couldn't tell Nicholas she didn't want him any more. She just couldn't.

He saw her distress and drew her into his arms, holding her tenderly against him. "I'm sorry to upset you, Kate."

She clung to him. "I'm thinking of Nicholas."

"I know. I've been thinking of him too. I've done nothing but think of you and him. But inside me I know that it wouldn't be right for you to marry him. You belong to me. You do, Kate, don't you?" She lifted a tear-stained face to him and he kissed her, buried his face in her rich dark hair, then kissed her again and again. Tears streamed down her cheeks but she didn't want him to stop kissing her.

"You told me you had no sleep last night, Kate, and neither did I. We must sleep tonight, and talk again when we can."

He held her close in his arms again as if he couldn't let her go, and then kissed her gently and tenderly again, wiping the tears from her face with his fingers. He looked deep into her eyes and then he whispered, "Goodnight, liebling," and softly left her room.

12

KATE lay in bed thinking about Nils and the next thing she knew it was morning and of course the first person in her thoughts was him and she hoped he'd slept as well as she had.

But then came remorse. How could she transfer her love to Nils? It was unthinkable. She didn't know him so how could she love him so much that he was the first person in her thoughts when she awoke?

But hadn't she always been in love with him? He was the one she was waiting for always. It was as if she'd known deep within her that he was waiting for her. She supposed it only happened to a few people so the majority wouldn't understand. Nicholas wouldn't understand. People would think so badly of her if she left him down.

But Nicholas understood more than she realised. There was a knock on the door and thinking it was Nils she called "Come in," and was surprised to see it was Nicholas.

"No, it's not Nils," he said, and came to sit on the side of her bed.

"What made you think I was expecting him?"

"Weren't you? I saw him leaving your room last night."

There was an almost tragic look in her eyes. She couldn't say a word.

"He didn't stay long, did he? Was that because you told him no?"

"He didn't ask," she said. "You were spying on me."

"Watching over you," he said. "Do you think I don't know that there's a great attraction between you two? It must be obvious to everyone. I saw him come to your room, I was watching out. I hung around in case you wanted me. What are you getting yourself into, sweetheart?"

"He simply wanted to speak to me.

He wanted to know if . . . " she paused, and then her face crumpled as she looked at Nicholas. "Oh, darling!"

He caught her to him and she cried on his chest. "I knew you were going to get hurt," he said. "It can't come to anything, my love."

"He said he would find a way to follow me."

"As bad as that, is it?" he smiled, gently. "I can't blame him, Kate. Are you going to let him take such a risk? Have you thought of the danger?"

"I couldn't let him risk his life. Perhaps I could stay here with him."

"Kate!" he exclaimed in a shocked voice. "You couldn't."

"That would be better than Nils getting shot trying to escape."

And then realising what she was saying and doing to Nicholas she clung to him again. "Oh, my dear, I feel so awful. I can't do this to you."

"It's you I'm thinking of, Kate," he said. "You've only been in each other's company a few hours."

"Perhaps it will pass. But you know, Nicholas, I've always known I was waiting for someone, and that's why I couldn't agree to marrying you. I couldn't understand it because I love you so much."

"Well now you've got all that off your chest I expect you feel better," he said, rising to his feet.

"No, I don't," she cried. "I feel awful."

"Don't distress yourself on my account, Kate," he said, patting her cheek. "You've got enough on your plate."

He saw Sharon on the roof garden and sat beside her. "Have you seen Nils this morning?" he asked.

"Yes," she said. "He's gone for a stroll before breakfast."

"I'm worried, Sharon," he said. "Nils is prepared to risk his life to follow Kate when she leaves."

"Oh, he wouldn't." said Sharon. "They could fall out of love as quickly as they fell in."

"Kate isn't the type to lose her head so completely. She didn't want it to happen, and she's worried over me. I don't want her to feel guilty about it. It's something she can't help."

"But she's bound to consider you," said Sharon.

"I don't want her to worry over me. I shall pretend that I'm falling in love with you and then she won't consider it necessary to have me on her conscience."

Sharon looked at him, troubled. She would do anything to help him, but he was asking a lot.

"When we go down we must look deep in conversation; it will help to give the impression that we are finding a lot in common and it will give credibility to our announcement when the time comes that we have fallen in love."

They were waiting to go into breakfast and all rose to go into the dining room when they saw Nicholas and Sharon approach.

Sharon had been feeling angry with

Kate for her treatment of Nicholas but when she saw the troubled look in her eyes as they rested on him, and the anxious look in Nils eyes too, she told herself she was judging too hastily. They weren't a couple of irresponsible children. Kate was twenty five and Nils nearly thirty. They were both concerned over what they were doing to Nicholas.

After breakfast Nicholas indicated that he would like to talk to Nils. They left the hotel and went for a walk. "I really ought to challenge you to a fight," said Nicholas. "You are trying to steal my girl."

Nils looked at him miserably. "If I were in your place I'd kill me," he said.

"This feeling between you and Kate can't lead to anything."

"I would risk anything for her."

"Have you thought what it would do to her if things went wrong?"

"She would have you to comfort her."

"Thanks," said Nicholas, in a dry voice.

"I'm thinking more of myself than I should," said Nils. "Would you fight me for Kate?"

"If that was what she wanted me to do."

"And if she chose me?"

"There would be no point in trying to keep her, Nils."

"She told me you have lived as husband and wife."

"Not really. We have slept together and I would have liked to become her husband. She agreed to marry me before we left England."

"I would not have tried to come between a man and his wife."

"We shall be only a few more days here," said Nicholas. "The decision is Kate's, but think carefully, Nils. Is it possible for you to get away from here?"

"I've never given such a thing a thought before," he said.

"Well make the best of the days that

are left before we leave. I can't advise you. I suppose if I were in your place I'd take risks, but it needs a lot of thought."

They returned to the hotel to find that Konrad was making plans to go to the Baltic coast. "The weather seems good today, but it will be getting colder as the summer draws to a close." he said.

They gathered their things together and when they went to the cars Nicholas turned to Kate and said, "You'd like to travel with Nils, wouldn't you?"

She looked at him in surprise and he gave her a little push. "Go on," he said. "Make the best of it."

When Nicholas entered Konrad's car he said, "I expect you've noticed that Kate and Nils have fallen hard for each other."

"Oh, Nicholas, no!" cried Frieda. "They couldn't have done."

"We are being very civilised about it, Kate and I," said Nicholas. "I have talked to both of them and there's no doubt about the way they feel about each other."

Sharon thought Nicholas was putting on a good face. He must be absolutely shattered, and yet he was making it easy for Nils and Kate to be together.

He turned to her, smiling. "Not to worry, Sharon. Things will turn out all right."

"You are very optimistic."

"No. Just prepared to let fate take its course."

As Kate sat beside Nils she said, "what were you and Nicholas talking about?"

"About you, of course," he said. "I thought he was going to challenge me to a fight. He loves you very much. He says the decision was left to you."

"Would it be possible for me to live in eastern Germany with you?"

"I wouldn't let you. It's never worried me because I've never particularly wanted to get away, but I wouldn't put you in that position. If we had children they would not be allowed to go to other parts of the world to live if they wanted."

"We needn't have children."

"We would want a family."

"Do people get away, Nils?" she asked.

"If they do we don't hear about it. It would give others ideas I suppose. Some have got away quite safely, no doubt."

"It's a terrible barrier."

"Well we won't think about it today," he said, "we'll enjoy ourselves."

She looked at him. He looked so much younger than Nicholas but there was a strength about him. She felt he would stop at nothing to get to her and it made her afraid. She tried to put all thoughts of danger out of her mind and enjoy being beside Nils. He was so wonderful she believed she was prepared to stay in this country just to be with him.

He told her there was some very valuable jewellery in his family. If they could get these gems out of the country as well as himself he could raise some money for them to live on until he found work to do.

He had really been thinking deeply. "In England I have a very nice flat," she said. "I have never wanted to share it with anyone, not even Nicholas. But you could share it with me."

He gave her a very loving look. "That is very kind of you. I shall get to you," and he reached out to grasp her hand.

He was driving towards Waremünde, a pleasing seaside resort, and she said, "Isn't there a way of escape by sea?"

"The bay is well protected," he said. "The authorities are not stupid."

"It's a pity I've come to spoil your contentment, Nils. You were happy enough with your family until I came along."

"Don't say that!" he protested. "You're the most wonderful thing that's ever happened to me. I've been transported into another world."

And the days that followed were wonderful. She was with Nils constantly and she felt so grateful to her friends for their sympathy and understanding. Most of all she was grateful to Nicholas who withdrew from her, allowing her the freedom she needed to be with Nils. The opportunities that gave the two of them to be alone, presented themselves all the time because of the understanding of the rest of the group.

Kate saw that Nicholas was giving a great deal of attention to Sharon and it pleased her. It was a help to him to have Sharon to turn to and Sharon deserved to have some attention. In France she had been concerned in case Sharon should be hurt by the behaviour of Nicholas, but now she was so involved with Nils she was glad to believe that Sharon was sensible enough not to allow herself to be hurt.

When she found herself alone in some wooded spot with Nils out of view from prying eyes all the world and everyone in it was forgotten as they embraced and murmured words of love to each other. Kate couldn't believe that this was her, so absolutely besotted. She had thought she knew what love was when she had been with Nicholas, but she hadn't. This was love. Being willing to belong to one's lover body and soul, not just when the fancy took one, but for all the time. Every minute of every day. Her life had been nothing before. How could she have believed herself happy before she met Nils?

To Sharon it seemed tragic that the love affair between Kate and Nicholas was over. She helped him, as he asked her, to make believe that a love affair was developing between them, but she knew it was only because Nicholas didn't want Kate to have to worry over hurting him. At times she felt that Nicholas went a little too far to try and convince the others that he didn't care. No one expected him to be able to give Kate up without a struggle, yet he always seemed in a good humour and even made Sharon laugh at times, telling her funny tales, and teasing her without mercy. Konrad too seemed to think it fun to pull her leg, but she took everything in good part.

The day before they were due to leave they paid another visit to Charlotte and her father. Charlotte told them she'd made the application for a permit for her and Herr Warneck to visit relations in West Germany, and that they were looking forward to paying them a visit in the near future.

When she knew that Nils and Kate had fallen in love she couldn't believe it. When Nils said he wanted to try and leave the country to be with Kate her anxiety showed. She was terribly afraid for her son.

"Nils doesn't think it a good idea for me to come and live in your country," said Kate.

"Neither do I," said his grandfather.

"They won't release me," said Nils.

My job is important. And if I asked for a permit to leave they'd keep an eye on me, perhaps."

They discussed nothing else. Frieda and Konrad were most concerned. They felt responsible for what had happened, yet were willing to suggest ways and means of getting Kate and Nils together. If Nicholas had accepted it they felt they could too.

It was agreed that they should get as much valuable jewellery out of the country as possible. Charlotte was even talking about the value of the items and Kate was surprised how soon she and her father had accepted the fact that Nils might be leaving them, never to be seen again.

"Nils doesn't have to worry," said Kate. "I have enough for both of us to live on."

"He wouldn't want to live on his wife's money," said Charlotte.

"We can take some valuables with us," said Herr Warneck. "Charlotte can wear rings and necklaces and we could look after them until Nils can collect them later; they would all go to him eventually, anyway."

"You think he could get out of the country?" asked Kate, with wide eyes.

"It's been done," he said. "I heard that a couple of guards were put on duty to guard a break in the concrete wall which was large enough for people to get through. One day they found the uniform of the two guards left behind, and the guards had disappeared through the wall."

"If only something as easy as that would crop up," laughed Kate.

"Some get help from people outside the country. They've taken them out hidden in lorries very ingeniously."

"There are reports in our papers now and again of daring escapes which had been successful, and people have asked for political asylum. A whole family got out once hidden in a huge tool box on a lorry. They had a frightening journey lasting about five hours, but managed to get through safely."

"They don't hesitate to shoot if they discover an escape," said Konrad. "It's no use thinking it can be done easily."

Kate shivered. "Oh, Nils, I'm scared."

"Let's pray to our guardian angels who brought us together," he smiled.

She held his arm, lovingly. He seemed so young and had the impulsiveness of youth. She hoped it wouldn't lead him into doing something foolhardy.

His mother, who had been upstairs, returned with a jewel box and they all began to admire the beautiful gems.

"We couldn't take them from you," said Kate.

"It's no great sacrifice for a mother to give all she's got to her son," said Charlotte. Kate was reduced to tears. She couldn't allow these people to have their lives disrupted like this.

But they all went on making plans. Frieda said that the three girls between them could wear rings and their items of jewellery when they left the country.

"And I'll take care of Charlotte," said her father.

"You mean I'll be taking care of you," she said. "I've spoilt you and Nils."

Frieda and Konrad said at last that they'd have to go back to their hotel. It was a tearful leave-taking. Sharon felt it was all like a dream. It couldn't possibly be happening. They had all accepted that Nils must be helped to get to Kate. Poor Nicholas. Impulsively she reached out and took his hand because they had become close over the past few days. He turned and gave her a smile and there was no great sorrow in his eyes. Maybe he felt that all this talk of escape and Nils and Kate getting together would end once they'd left, and everything would get back to normal.

The old man had taken to Kate very strongly and he gave her a hug before she left and Kate kissed him on the cheek. She saw there were tears in his eyes and she clung to him a little before releasing herself.

Nils insisted on accompanying them

back to the hotel for he wanted to be with Kate until the very last minute. But neither of them could speak for some time when they got in the car and moved away to follow the others.

He turned at last to see that tears were streaming down her face. "Oh, Kate!" he exclaimed.

"We're being stupid," she said. "We've taken leave of our senses. We can't worry other people as we're doing."

"I know how you feel, Kate," he said. "But I feel we must make a bid for our happiness. I'd rather take a chance on being with you than having to go on without you."

"Wait awhile after I've left. See if you change your mind when I'm not there."

"You know I couldn't change."

The others arrived back at the hotel before them and had retired to their rooms. It seemed the most natural thing in the world for Kate and Nils to go hand in hand to her room. It was unthinkable that they should separate until the very last minute.

Kate gave herself wholly and irrevocably to Nils. They didn't sleep all night. Nicholas had told her many times that she only wanted him to give her sexual satisfaction. She cared about him more than she cared about herself. It wasn't only sex they wanted from each other. Side by side they lay talking and talking, wanting to learn all they could about each other. Then they would cling to each other, hating the thought that in the morning they had to part, perhaps never to see each other again.

She knew that Nils was not an experienced lover. He had a lot to learn but that didn't matter. It was Nils she loved, and that was more important. She would have loved him forever even if they hadn't spent this last night together. This just added to their joy in each other. She knew she would never tell him that she wanted to be alone, as she'd told Nicholas, little dreaming how much she must have hurt him, until now she was really in love herself. Nicholas was wiser than she had given him credit for. He had known her love wasn't the real thing as far as he was concerned.

When the dawn came the tears began to stream down her face. Nils wiped them away and kissed her cheeks, assuring her that everything would be all right. This was not goodbye. They would see each other again.

He left her room before people began to stir and Kate was left with emptiness. Soon they wouldn't even be in the same building, and then not even in the same country. She was afraid of showing distress. Who knows whether some officious person might notice that a visitor from the West had taken a fancy to someone from the East and keep a watch on them.

It should have been Nicholas looking pale and strained, for hadn't he lost his fiancée? But it was Nils who looked dreadful. Perhaps Nicholas didn't believe he had lost her completely. Maybe he thought the affair would peter out once they left this country. Talking about escape was different from actually doing something about it.

Kate left everything to the others when it came to leave-taking. She simply couldn't think straight. Nils came to her room for a final leave-taking and they clung to each other. They couldn't break apart.

He kissed every part of her face and she felt her heart was breaking. Supposing she never saw him again. How could she bear it? But she had to go. They were waiting for her. She gave him a final kiss, and then unable to speak, she fled, knowing that her tearful flight attracted attention from hotel guests.

Nicholas had assured Nils that he would look after her which was amazing to the others, particularly Sharon who knew what a strong bond there had been between him and Kate. There was no bitterness in him at all. He took control of Kate, sat between her and Sharon in the back of the car. Sharon and Kate were crying, for Sharon couldn't see Kate in such a state without being affected too. Nicholas told them in a stern voice to pull themselves together.

"You must hate me, Nicholas," sobbed Kate.

"How could I hate you?" he said.

13

SAFELY back in the West they all gave a sigh of relief because without any trouble at all they had brought out a few thousand pounds worth of jewellery, either being worn, or packed in their cases. That part of the plan had gone successfully.

Kate would have been hopeless without the others to take control in getting to the airport, and back to the Ehler's castle. She was like someone bereaved.

Their journey over, Nicholas insisted that Kate had something to eat and then went to bed. She looked frightful. He guessed she'd had no sleep all night, and nothing to eat all day. "If you don't look after yourself," he warned her, "it will be no use Nils trying to reach you. You're going to fade away."

During the last few days in East Germany Sharon had had a great deal of attention from Nicholas, but now he was helping Kate to endure the ordeal of waiting day after day for Nils to come to her. In spite of that he managed to make Sharon feel important to him, and she had to keep reminding herself that this was simply for Kate's benefit to take away her feeling of guilt. How could Kate have accepted help from Nicholas if he had shown that he was heartbroken over losing her love?

Sharon often discovered Kate watching her and Nicholas. Perhaps she was wondering if Nicholas was really lost to her. Supposing Nils didn't manage to get to her. Would Nicholas be prepared to marry her now that he knew her love belonged to another man? Kate must have been thinking along those lines, thought Sharon. Her life would be extremely empty if she had neither Nicholas or Nils.

They all seemed to have been drawn to Frieda and Konrad Ehlers because of this affair so that it seemed quite natural to accept their invitation to stay on a little longer to see how things might turn out. Sharon wrote to her parents to tell them they were staying longer than expected. She had suggested that she return to England, but Kate and Nicholas wouldn't hear of it.

"You're not travelling back alone," said Nicholas. "Besides, Kate needs you as much as she needs me," which was true.

Sharon liked to think she was giving some comfort to Nicholas because he had lost his love, but he didn't seem to be seeking comfort from her. He made it appear that he wanted to be in her company more and more.

"What about our partnership, Nicholas?" asked Kate.

"Is there any reason why we shouldn't continue to work together?" he queried.

"You mean you would like to go on working with me in spite of what I've done to you?"

"Don't talk like that. Nothing has really changed, has it?" he asked. "I knew you didn't love me as I did you. But we have always enjoyed working together and I don't see why we shouldn't continue. It would be a shame to break up a good partnership, even if you and Nils were lucky enough to get together. We could all be good friends as we've been over here."

"It's been a splendid and profitable partnership," she admitted.

"In more ways than one," he smiled.

"Nicholas, you've been wonderful to me," she said. "I can't understand myself. I really can't."

"Well don't try. Just to put it down to mysterious powers at work."

He rose and gave her a kiss and went in search of Sharon. "Kate's not going to break up the partnership whatever happens," he said, looking very satisfied about it.

To pass the time away Frieda and Konrad thought of all sorts of things to keep them occupied. They went shopping in Dusseldorf to get warmer clothing, for the days were becoming cooler. They paid a visit to their hunting lodge which was situated between Cologne and Dusseldorf and it was a beautiful place.

Before they went shopping Nicholas insisted on giving Sharon some money to get herself some really special clothes. The colour rushed to her face and she was about to refuse it, but he stopped her. "You are placed in a situation you didn't expect and I don't want you to be embarrassed in any way." He gave her a hug, and went on. "I want to see what you buy. You have excellent taste."

And he went with her into her room to examine all the lovely things she bought while she was shopping with Kate and Frieda. She had never had so much money to spend on herself, and as he said, she had excellent taste. He held up the dresses she'd bought and teasingly asked her if he was going to be allowed to see her try them on.

"You're not," she said. "You'll have to wait until I'm wearing them before you see what I look like."

"You're a spoilsport," he told her, and she found herself pulled into his arms and given a kiss which seemed to reach to all parts of her body.

"Nicholas," she gasped, dreamy eyed. "What are you doing to me?"

"What are you doing to me?" he grinned. "I suppose it would be safer if I left you to try those things on alone."

There were other occasions when they were staying at the hunting lodge that Nicholas managed to steal a kiss and it wasn't always for Kate's benefit. The lodge was set in deep woods where there was a natural game park with red and fallow deer, roe and wild boar. When they wandered through these delightful grounds they seemed to be in a world of make-believe, at least Sharon did, and when Nicholas acted like some prince, treating her as if she were a fine lady, she fell in with the pretence and accepted his kisses, knowing how much she would miss them when they were back in England.

More and more he managed to be at her side wherever they went and she couldn't believe it was all necessary for Kate's benefit. Kate was like someone in a trance at times and Sharon was sure that she was thinking of no one but Nils. They knew she must be lying awake night after night worrying, because there were dark shadows beneath her eyes. Nothing anyone could do would make Kate feel any better. The only person who could do that was Nils, and if he escaped it would be a miracle.

14

BACK in East Germany Nils had not given up thoughts of escape but as yet couldn't think of a safe way of getting out of the country.

His grandfather sat thinking about Nils, wishing he could accompany him and his mother when they left the country. Several times he said. "I wish you'd go in my place. I've had my life. You know some people in the theatrical world. They could help you make up to look old like me."

Nils laughed at him. "I know I resemble you but it would be impossible to make me look as old as you are. There are fifty years difference in our ages. And I couldn't leave you behind to suffer for allowing me to use your papers."

"I haven't much time left to me, anyway, Nils."

But Nils felt his grandfather's suggestion was too fanciful to be successful, even if he could take advantage of his generosity.

He prayed desperately every night that he would find a way. There had to be some way he could get his freedom. Soon his mother and his grandfather would be leaving for the West and he wanted them to be able to tell Kate he was making plans, but he didn't have any at the moment. Again and again his grandfather tried to persuade him to do as he suggested, but Nils said there must be some other way.

"You would only have to stoop a little, put on an old man's clothes, and you'd look older right away." said Herr Warneck. "A couple of days' growth of beard and my spectacles. The weather seems cold to old people now. You could wrap a woollen scarf round your neck, and wear woollen gloves to hide the fact that your hands are young. You could do it," the old man kept arguing, and Nils got impatient with him.

The letter telling Konrad and Frieda when they would be arriving had already been forwarded. What would they think if Nils allowed his grandfather to stay behind and face the consequences of allowing Nils to travel in his place even if he could get away with it?

On a Sunday morning, two days before their departure, Nils was having breakfast with his mother. He was feeling depressed because he couldn't send a hopeful message to Kate and told his mother she had better tell her to forget him and go back to Nicholas.

Charlotte was sorry for him. She would have given anything to see him happily married to the girl he wanted so badly. She rose to pour some tea and asked him to take a cup to his grandfather.

Nils rose and took it upstairs. The old man was fast asleep. Nils put the tea on the bedside cabinet. He turned to look at him. It was a shame to wake him for a cup of tea. He was lying very still and something about the silence in the room gave Nils a strange feeling. He bent over his grandfather, carefully, not wishing to startle him, but he suspected that nothing would startle his beloved grandpa again. He moved the sheet and touched his hands. They were very cold.

Nils was terribly shocked. He knew there was no life there. He had been perfectly all right when he went to bed and Nils stood looking at him. His mother would be heartbroken. This was so sudden and unexpected.

He turned away to go down and tell his mother when his eye caught something on the bedside cabinet. It was an empty bottle. Nils looked at his grandfather in awe. Had he killed himself? If he had it was for one reason only. He wanted Nils to go to Western Germany in his place. "Oh, no, grandpa," he cried, and knelt beside the bed in tears.

He put the bottle in his pocket.

He wouldn't tell his mother what he suspected grandpa had done. Was it his imagination, or was there a smile on the old man's face? A smile which seemed to say, "You have your chance now," and he looked so happy and peaceful.

His death was not such a great shock to Charlotte after all. "I have noticed how weary he was getting. I was worried about him travelling in case it would be too much for him."

And looking upon his face with such a happy expression she couldn't be upset for long. It was a blessing he had gone without suffering.

Nils said he would have to ring the doctor, but before he had got out of the room she stopped him. "No, Nils!" she cried. "Don't tell anyone. Your grandfather has insisted so many times that you could get out with his papers, but we couldn't allow him to be left to take the consequences. Now he can't come to any harm and his idea is worth thinking about. He would help you if he could."

"The guards give close scrutiny to everyone leaving the country," he said. "How could I get away with it?" But already he was thinking of ways and means.

"We will make grandfather look beautiful and leave him here," said Charlotte. "You have the same coloured eyes, the same features. A grey wig and a couple of days' growth of beard would make you look more like him."

"His beard is grey."

"You would have to use some bleach."

"His eyes are wrinkled, and his eyebrows grey."

"You could wear his glasses. Screw up your eyes Nils and let me look at you."

He did so and she said, "your eyes are swollen at the moment because you've been upset, that makes them look bleary. It's a pity you couldn't make them look like that and with your beard and eyebrows bleached, a grey wig and his clothes, you'd look very much like your grandpa."

Nils thought about it and decided it was worth a try. He knew a girl who worked at the theatre. Perhaps she could find a grey wig for him from the make-up room. He decided to go right away for they often rehearsed on Sundays.

But when he arrived the theatre was closed. He walked around the side, saw a small low window leading to a toilet or broom cupboard. He made sure there was no one around and with fast beating heart was able to open it with his penknife and slip inside. It had been easier than he expected.

Quickly, feeling like a criminal, he ran up the stairs to the dressing rooms and after looking around came upon many models of heads with wigs perched upon them. There was a grey one. He lifted it and tried it on, looking at himself in the mirror. He was surprised to find how firmly it sat on his head. It could be combed and arranged as he wanted, so trembling with fear and excitement he grabbed it off his head and fled with it. He was out of the building in a shot. His heart didn't stop thumping until he was well away from the theatre and he knew he'd got away unobserved.

Back home he tried it on and his mother combed it and styled it in the way her father had worn his hair. He tried on his grandfather's clothes, put on his spectacles, stooped as if with age and gradually saw the transformation taking place. He had two days to let his beard grow and he began to think that he had a chance. The men at the checkpoint wouldn't know his grandfather and if he could make himself look like his photograph he might just get away with it.

On the Monday morning Nils went to work. He didn't want to give any cause for suspicion. He hadn't shaved, but no one spoke about it. Being in the chemistry department he had access to bleach and also a solution that would make his eyes sore and bleary. He could hardly concentrate on his work knowing that tomorrow he would either be out of the country for good, or possibly he would have been shot or taken by guards to prison. He couldn't allow himself to think of the joy that would be his if his escape was successful.

By the end of the day it was very obvious that he was in need of a shave. He got away as soon as he could, as much for his mother's sake as his own for she had been left all day in the house with his grandfather lying in state upstairs.

As soon as Nils got home he began to work on his disguise, bleaching his beard and eyebrows, trying the solution in his eyes to make them watery and the lids swollen. Both he and his mother were too tense to eat anything.

They intended to travel by train as Charlotte would have done with her father. There would be several stops before they reached the border and they could only hope that they met no one who knew them well.

It was going to be absolutely nerve-wracking and Nils knew he would feel hot and uncomfortable wearing a wig and all the woollen clothes his mother had put for him to wear. His grandfather would have worn them, and they would help to give the impression he was old.

He wore his grandfather's stout sensible shoes which pinched a little and made him walk stiffly which wasn't a bad thing. They went to take a last look at Herr Warneck before leaving and dared not allow themselves to think about leaving him behind to be discovered goodness knows when. Nils had tried to make himself believe that he had not taken an overdose of tablets.

They sneaked out of the house like

a couple of thieves, dreading in case one of their neighbours should stop to speak to them, and then they were away to the railway station. Nils parked the car. They got on to the train without seeing anyone they knew, and then began that nerve-wracking train journey to the border.

Nils thought his mother was wonderful to be taking this risk with him. Once they were away, if they managed it, she would have time to think about her father and would grieve over him. Perhaps this little escapade had helped her in a way to accept his death more easily than she might have done. Nils kept reminding himself that she had told him that she'd been expecting the end for the old man, though he hadn't noticed himself that he was cracking up.

How they sat in the train without panic he would never know. The train was slowing up for the final stage. The border was in sight and soon they would know their fate.

The suspense was absolutely killing. Charlotte glanced at her son. Would she have been taken in by such a disguise if she hadn't known Nils was her son? No one had seemed to think there was anything suspicious about his appearance.

The train was pulling up and Charlotte knew she had to be very very strong. Her own performance as they crossed the border was every bit as important as Nils's.

When they left the train Nils took his mother's arm and could feel her shaking. Those in authority were checking the people very carefully as they passed through. They had to pass this test and must be careful to remember they were supposed to be father and daughter.

In trying to give strength to his mother Nils found strength himself. He held her arm so strongly she gradually stopped shaking. He had practised in the mirror looking old and discovered that if he held his mouth tight and let it fall at the outer edges it gave him an older look. With his two days growth of beard, bleary eyes, a grey wig falling a little untidily and his grandfather's clothing, he had a good chance of getting through. He screwed up his eyes a little to make them crinkle at the sides. And he tried not to think that anything could go wrong.

He held his handkerchief to his nose most of the time and at last, when it was their turn to hand in their papers, he began to sniffle and snuffle, dabbing at his eyes and nose. The young man looked at him in disgust.

He studied the papers, looked at Nils and said, curtly, "Take off your glasses."

Nils fumbled and shook as he took them off and peered at him with swollen painful eyes. He looked into a pair of cold heartless eyes and the possessor of them walked away. He began to talk to another official and Nils and Charlotte were holding their breath. Had they suspected anything?

The other man turned and lifted a telephone receiver. Their hearts sank. Something was wrong. He began talking away but they couldn't hear what he was saying. Then he returned to the man who was dealing with them, said something they couldn't hear and they both began to laugh. Nils had put on the glasses again now and when the official came back he looked at him with distaste as he handed the papers to Charlotte and allowed them to go through.

With no signs of elation Nils and his mother went on their way to collect their luggage and board a train in the Western sector. It was unbelievable that they were through. They couldn't speak. They were still terrified. Afraid they would be called back, or they would feel a hand on their shoulders and ordered to stop!

Their feet hardly seemed to touch the ground as they walked on and no one approached them. Even when they were on the train travelling in the Western sector they couldn't believe it. They were not travelling alone and even now Nils didn't feel safe enough to take off the heavy-rimmed glasses. He was just waiting until they arrived at Frankfurt am Main in order that he could cast off his disguise and give a whoop of joy.

Little smiles kept forcing their way to Charlotte's face. She was longing to laugh but was still afraid to show her feelings. She opened her bag and produced some sandwiches for neither of them had eaten for hours. They hadn't been able to think of food. Now they began to relax and felt marvellous after having had something to eat.

When their carriage emptied he dared to take off the spectacles to turn to his mother with a huge smile. She laughed, for he looked a dreadful sight, but gradually his eyes were looking less painful.

"It's amazing how the years have

dropped off you since we boarded this train," she said.

He started to laugh and so did she and they laughed and laughed almost hysterically. They had done it. They had done it.

15

BACK at Ehler's castle there was
an air of expectancy. They had
no idea, of course, that Nils
would be arriving in his grandfather's
place. But they were looking forward
to seeing Charlotte and her father, Kate
particularly, as she was dying for news
from Nils.

Sharon and Nicholas were making
preparations to return to England for
there was no point in hanging on after
they'd seen Charlotte unless they had
plans for Nils to get out of the country
with help from outside. Nicholas was
willing to help if he could.

Sharon was anxious to go home now.
It was a strain being with Nicholas all
the time, pretending they were falling
in love. He gave her some very loving,
tender looks at times and she felt like
hitting him. Couldn't he imagine what

effect he was having on her? It might be funny to him but it wasn't to her.

Konrad set off to pick up their guests while Frieda stayed behind to supervise a welcoming meal for them.

Kate walked restlessly from room to room wondering what news Charlotte would have for her. Would she tell her to give up all hopes of seeing her son again? Had they realised it was senseless to try and get away? If it meant living in his country with him Kate would do so. She didn't care what anyone said, she wanted to be with Nils wherever he was.

Soon Nicholas would be on his way to England and that made her feel wretched. They had meant so much to each other. Yet she remembered the feeling she had had when he took her to see the house in Surrey. Something had told her that she would never live there with Nicholas.

And Nicholas had been so good to her. He'd even told her he would try to contact someone in England who could plan a way of escape for Nils.

While they were hanging about for Konrad to return Charlotte and Nils were being driven towards the castle. Konrad had listened in astonishment as they told him how they'd tricked the officials. He hadn't immediately recognised Nils, but he had known it wasn't Herr Warneck. How lucky they'd been to get away with it. It was sad about Herr Warneck and now Nils could think about it more. It had been on his mind, and he couldn't forget that empty bottle, and yet he had a feeling the old man was near to him, happy for him, and he owed it to him to be happy and make Kate happy.

"Let the others see you in your disguise," laughed Konrad. "Let's see their reaction."

And so Nils, still muffled in the scarf, gloves and hat, shuffled into the large hall, his eyes hidden by his grandfather's glasses, and waited for the result. They all knew immediately that he was not Herr Warneck. Charlotte was beaming at them all and it was Kate who realised first that Nils was standing there before her and she gave a squeal of joy as she ran forward. "Nils! Nils! It is you. I know it's you!"

He snatched off the wig and all the other paraphernalia to hug her in his arms and he swung her round and round in excitement.

She drew her hands down his face to make sure it really was him and he said, "I'll soon get rid of this," fingering his hairy chin, "and I'd like to bathe my eyes. I had to use something to make them run and my eye lids swell."

To sadden this glad occasion they had to hear of the death of his grandfather. Such a grand old man. So alert for his age. "He would be so happy to know that Nils got away safely," said Charlotte, and Nils knew he would be forever grateful to him in his heart. He couldn't tell anyone that he feared his life had been given in order that Nils could start a new one.

He couldn't wait now to get out of the crippling shoes he was wearing, take a shave, cast away the wig and get back to normal. His eyebrows were going to look a bit queer until the natural colour came back to them, but his eyes were already feeling less painful. Fortunately Konrad's clothes were his size and he went off upstairs for a bath and a change of clothing to emerge shortly afterwards looking more himself.

They could talk of nothing else for ages except the wonderful escape and listened to Charlotte and then Nils telling how they felt as they were stopped at the border. "When grandpa suggested I used his papers to get away it seemed too fantastic for words," said Nils, "and yet it came off."

Kate was shaking with excitement. She didn't leave his side for a moment, and he kept his arm around her, pausing to give her little kisses on the side of her face now and again as he talked.

They were all sorts of things to talk

about now he was free. Their marriage, his plans for the future, which were to start a research laboratory if he could, in England. He wouldn't be short of friends to help him.

But those things could wait. They could see that it had all been overwhelming for Charlotte who begged to be allowed to go to bed. And it was obvious that Kate and Nils wanted to be alone so no one minded when Kate took him up to her room. They could all imagine what was happening there. Kate in Nils' arms receiving long satisfying kisses with no fears for the future. They were together and didn't have to part again. "I've been so scared," said Kate, "so I don't know how you felt actually taking the risk you did."

"I would have dared anything for you," he smiled.

Kate felt that he was already her husband after spending that night with him, yet she had never felt that way about Nicholas after all the nights

269

he'd spent with her. There were no doubts at all when the question of marriage arose between her and Nils. "We must be married as soon as possible," he said.

"As soon as you like," she promised.

When Kate and Nils rejoined the others, much, much later, they still seemed to be in a dream. But Nicholas wanted to talk to Kate about some valuable works of art Konrad had generously given them to take back to England with them, and she told Konrad how grateful they were.

"We have a good business going, Nils," said Nicholas. "Will you object to Kate carrying on with me in partnership as before?"

"If that is what Kate wants," said Nils.

"You could work with us too, if you wished."

Sharon listened in amazement. How could Nicholas contemplate working with the man who had stolen his love from him?

"It's good of you to offer," said Nils, "but if possible I would like to continue doing the work I'm used to. I like it."

That night Sharon lay in bed thinking about the journey to England tomorrow. There would be just her and Nicholas. Perhaps once Nicholas was away from Kate he would feel free to expose his feelings. It would upset her to see him unhappy.

Everyone seemed sorry they were leaving the next morning, Kate clung to Nicholas with tears in her eyes and he gave her a big hug. "You don't have to have me on your conscience, does she Sharon?" he said, taking her hand and pulling her close to his side. "Sharon and I are going to be married."

The astonishment in Kate's eyes was no more than that in Sharon's. This was carrying things too far, but Nicholas went on regardless. "You must have seen, all of you how it was between Sharon and I. I wouldn't have broken our engagement but when I could see you didn't care for me Kate, you couldn't blame me for going for beautiful Sharon."

"Oh, darling, Nicholas!" exclaimed Kate. "Oh, I'm so happy for you and you, Sharon. I'm thrilled for you both. Nothing will please me more than to see you and Nicholas together. That's all I needed to complete my own happiness. You've always thought a lot of Nicholas, haven't you, Sharon?"

Sharon smiled with great difficulty. "We wanted to see you and Nils safely together before announcing our plans," she said, managing to give Nicholas a deadly look over Kate's shoulder as she came to give her a kiss.

He had no right to put her in this position just to give Kate peace of mind. How did he think it made her feel? Or weren't her feelings important? He knew very well they'd made no such plans and it would make her look as if she'd been jilted when Kate learned that no marriage was to take place.

Nicholas saw her anger, and he laughed. She could have killed him.

16

IT was not often that Sharon got really angry. And she'd never imagined she could ever possibly be angry with Nicholas. But she was now. There wasn't much she could do about it either until they were alone. What was more infuriating was the fact that he was aware of her anger and it amused him. He wouldn't be amused when she got the chance to tell him what she thought about him.

Kate came to her room as she checked that she had all her bits and pieces and was leaving nothing behind. "I am happy for you, Sharon," she said. "Nicholas is quite a guy. He wasn't particularly heartbroken over my giving him up, was he? I think he stopped loving me even as far back as when we were in France. I caught him kissing you, remember? He said he thought it was me, but did he?" Kate was beaming at her.

"Oh, Kate!" said Sharon. "Nicholas would have always remained true to you."

"I think he would have done because he wouldn't have wanted to hurt me. I hated to hurt him too. He wants someone to love him as I love Nils, or as you love him."

Sharon might have admitted that she loved him desperately if she hadn't been so angry with him.

Konrad was driving her and Nicholas to the airport and Sharon was almost in tears when everyone came to wish them goodbye as they left the castle.

"A good thing Nils made it out of the East," said Nicholas. "I think Kate would have gone to him if he hadn't been able to get to her and we should have all hated that."

"Nils more than anyone," said Konrad. "He couldn't have let her do that for him."

"I hope they get everything sorted

274

out satisfactorily," said Nicholas. "I'm sure he'll find protection in England."

They arrived at the airport and Konrad remained with them until their flight was called. Sharon was beginning to see the likeness between Konrad and his cousin. They were both nicer than she had ever imagined Germans could be.

The weather was blustery and Sharon was not so confident as she was when they set off from England, how long ago? It seemed they'd spent a life time in Germany.

Nicholas wanted to hold her hand to give her courage as he'd done on their very first flight together, but she shrugged him off. Even though she was scared she was too angry with him to let him fuss around her.

"You're absolutely seething, aren't you?" he said. "We're going to have a good talk, you and I. But this is not the right time."

It wasn't. She realised that as the wind buffetted the plane. Not used to travelling she found it most nerve-wracking, especially when they were told not to unfasten their seat belts because of turbulence. She was glad to have Nicholas by her side in spite of her anger with him.

Nicholas ordered a brandy for her and insisted that she drank it. "You needn't think I'm willing to be softened up to forgive you for making that announcement," she said.

"Hush," he said, and then turned to smile at her. "It's not a bad thing is it? For us to get married?"

He couldn't mean that, surely? Was he actually willing to go through with it? Perhaps it had hurt his pride being turned down in front of everyone like that and he wanted to salve some of it by letting everyone think it wasn't important, that he had someone else to turn to.

It was too bumpy a flight for them to relax sufficiently for conversation and he said, "Leave it. We'll talk, I promise you."

Everyone on the plane was thankful when they landed safely at Heathrow. Nicholas took control of everything and told Sharon to stay put while he fetched his car which had been left on the car park far longer than they had expected it to be.

As Sharon watched him go she felt proud that she knew such a smart looking man. And was he serious when he said it wasn't a bad thing for them to get married? He couldn't really mean it. If he did, would she agree, knowing how much Kate meant to him? The thought of marrying Nicholas was too wonderful to comtemplate.

When they were ready to drive away from the airport Sharon didn't notice at first which direction he was taking. He didn't enter into conversation and she sat silently beside him. Perhaps he was angry with her now and wouldn't discuss marriage or anything else, but would drop her at her home. And that would be that. But then she noticed that he wasn't going in the direction of her home.

"Where are you taking me?" she asked.

"I told you we were going to talk. We're going to my flat. I don't know whether you're hungry but I am. I rang through to tell my daily woman, Mrs Carter, what time we'd be back approximately and she's preparing a meal for us."

He turned to give her a smile and her heart turned over. He didn't know what he did to her.

His flat was quite different from Kate's. It was obvious that there was no shortage of money when it had been furnished, but it had a masculine air about it. Kate's had an air of luxury and femininity. Nicholas's flat was serviceable, with all comforts provided but not so showily.

He greeted his daily, introduced her to Sharon, and then in spite of her presence drew Sharon into his bedroom. "I know you are dying to have a go at me, Sharon," he said. "But if I had thought for one moment that you didn't want to marry me I wouldn't have made that announcement."

"How could you know I wanted to marry you?" she asked, taken aback.

"I've seen that look in your eyes when they've rested on me, and you've been concerned over Kate giving me up. You couldn't have cared that much if you didn't love me yourself."

The colour rose to her face. "You think I would be contented with a husband who loved someone else?"

"No. I wouldn't expect you to be."

"Well!"

"Well!" he mimicked her. "I couldn't tell you I loved you until I was sure Kate was settled. She will always mean a lot to me and I always hoped that we should marry. I'm not a man who likes sleeping around. I wanted Kate to be my wife. You knew that. When it became obvious that she didn't care enough for me to want to marry me my feelings changed. Love had to be reciprocated. When we talked about making her jealous I knew in my heart that I didn't want to have to go to such lengths to make Kate love me. I had already come to accept that it was no use. Kate didn't want me as I wanted her. When she thought I was interested in you she agreed to marry me. But it was too late then, I was already in love with you."

"You mean when we were in France?" she asked, incredulously.

"Yes. I was jealous when you were having fun with those young men on the beach. And when Jules came to claim your attention. And I knew why I was jealous. I think Kate must have suspected too because she agreed to marry me. She didn't want me, yet she didn't want to let me go."

"So I wasted my time being sorry for you in Germany," she retorted.

"No, you didn't," he smiled. "You were making me fall deeper and deeper in love with you. But I felt under an obligation to stick by Kate until the last minute. You don't mind if I tell you I'll always care about her? She's a beautiful, wonderful person, but she wasn't for me. I want you, Sharon. I shall be happier with you."

"I suppose I could put up with being second best, Nicholas. I love you so very much. It's unbelievable that you should ask me to take Kate's place, but I will, I daresay, when I've got used to the idea. I can't imagine myself becoming your wife, it seems too marvellous to be true."

He gave her a shake. "You haven't been listening to me," he said. "You won't be second best. I love you, Sharon. I'm glad that Kate is fixed up with Nils because I would have gone on and married her, even though I knew I'd fallen in love with you. I love you with all my heart. You've got to believe that."

Tears began to spill down her face and he pulled her into his arms and held her close. "I do love you," he insisted. "Really. And you've admitted you love me. We will get married?"

"Do you think I'd make a suitable wife for you? To live with you in that beautiful house you took me to see?"

"I've been picturing you there with me all the time. Ever since I bought it. I could see that you loved it as much as I did as soon as I saw it. And Kate was quite indifferent. It left her untouched. It was so disappointing to know that I would be living there with her and she couldn't have cared less about the house. I wished then that I could have told her that it didn't matter if she didn't want me, that I would be happier with you. But I knew I was important to Kate as a lover."

She lifted her face to give him a kiss and he enfolded her in his arms to give her the most devastating kiss she could ever imagine. She felt herself floating away, yet even so she wondered if she would be able to satisfy him sexually as Kate had done.

They became so passionate it seemed that she was going to be put to the test there and then, but Nicholas released her and smiled tenderly into her eyes. "How soon do we get married?" he asked.

"As soon as you like," she told him.

"Fine," he said. "It would be today if I could arrange it."

"I expect you have missed sleeping with Kate. I hope I will be . . . "

He stopped her. "Will you stop that? Don't compare yourself with Kate. I shall not be thinking of Kate when I make love to you, Sharon. You must believe that."

"She's so beautiful."

"And so are you. I'll be furious with you if you keep comparing yourself with Kate and believe that I'm making comparisons too. Do you know why I said I wouldn't sleep with Kate again until we were married? It was because I didn't feel I wanted to make love to her when I loved you instead?"

"It's just that everything seems so wonderful. I can't believe that this is happening to me, Nicholas."

"Life has seemed like a dream for months, hasn't it? First in France where I first began to feel drawn to you. I never imagined I could fall out of love with Kate, but you made me fall in love with you."

"I didn't." she protested. "I knew all along you belonged to Kate."

"That's what you thought. Belonged is in the past tense. Another girl would have made the most of her opportunities you know. I gave you plenty of chances to fall into my arms, but you didn't. A very loyal person you are. I know you're fond of Kate, and that's mutual, but you never thought about yourself and what you wanted."

"Well, neither did you," said Sharon. "You put Kate first, not yourself."

"Stupid pair, aren't we?" he grinned. "Come on, love, we'll go and see what Mrs Carter has prepared for us. Did she say roast duck?"

"I was too preoccupied to notice

284

what she said when we came in," said Sharon.

"Too busy hating me," he smiled. "But you can't be indifferent to some people. You either hate them or you love them. Now just be sure you always love me," he ordered, turning her round to go into the dining room.

Sharon could have been eating sawdust and it would have tasted wonderful. She tried to picture herself and Nicholas dining like this in that wonderful house in the country. How she had envied Kate having the chance to live there. But she'd given all that up and Nicholas for Nils. What people will do for love.

She knew that her parents would be anxious to see her after being away for so long. But Nicholas couldn't let her go so soon. He kept her talking, sitting with his arm around her, reluctant to lose the intimacy of being alone with her like this.

Eventually they got round to seeing her parents, telling them all the news which they found as difficult to believe as Sharon had found it to learn that Nicholas loved her. They heard all about what had happened to Kate and Sharon's father wanted to know what would happen now Nils had managed to get to her.

"The greatest hurdle has been overcome," said Nicholas. "He's free and I have no doubt he will receive lots of help. My main concern now is myself and Sharon. We want to be married very soon."

And they were. There was no great publicity as there would have been if he'd been marrying Kate, but he didn't want that and neither did Sharon. They just wanted a quiet wedding, and then to be together all the time. Nicholas would not agree to their spending nights together until the ring was on her finger. He wanted to do the right thing this time.

It wasn't long before Kate returned to England with Nils. He proved to be a quick worker and before long had that research laboratory of his own which he had always longed for. It was great to know they were back in England and the four of them remained close friends.

Before long Sharon had settled into her new home and was running it so well one would have thought she'd been born to that sort of life.

When Kate announced that she was going to have a baby when they came visiting, Sharon saw Nicholas look a little wistful. She knew he would love to have a family. But she had some good news for him too. She hadn't had time to tell him yet. It could wait until they were alone. He had to be the first to know.

HOSPITAL BY THE LAKE
Anne Durham

Nurse Marguerite Ingleby was always ready to become personally involved with her patients, to the despair of Brian Field, the Senior Surgical Registrar, who loved her.

VALLEY OF CONFLICT
David Farrell

Isolated in a hostel in the French Alps, Ann Russell sees her fiancé being seduced by a young girl. Then comes the avalanche that imperils their lives.

NURSE'S CHOICE
Peggy Gaddis

A proposal of marriage from the incredibly handsome and wealthy Reagan was enough to upset any girl — and Brooke Martin was no exception.

A DANGEROUS MAN
Anne Goring

Photographer Polly Burton was on safari in Mombasa when she met enigmatic Leon Hammond. But unpredictability was the name of the game where Leon was concerned.

PRECIOUS INHERITANCE
Joan Moules

Karen's new life working for an authoress took her from Sussex to a foreign airstrip and a kidnapping; to a real life adventure as gripping as any in the books she typed.

VISION OF LOVE
Grace Richmond

When Kathy takes over the rundown country kennels she finds Alec Stinton, a local vet, very helpful. But their friendship arouses bitter jealousy and a tragedy seems inevitable.

DOCTOR NAPIER'S NURSE
Pauline Ash

When cousins Midge and Derry are entered as probationer nurses on the same day but at different hospitals they agree to exchange identities.

A GIRL LIKE JULIE
Louise Ellis

Caroline absolutely adored Hugh Barrington, but then Julie Crane came into their lives. Julie was the kind of girl who attracts men without even trying.

COUNTRY DOCTOR
Paula Lindsay

When Evan Richmond bought a practice in a remote country village he did not realise that a casual encounter would lead to the loss of his heart.

ENCORE
Helga Moray

Craig and Janet realise that their true happiness lies with each other, but it is only under traumatic circumstances that they can be reunited.

NICOLETTE
Ivy Preston

When Grant Alston came back into her life, Nicolette was faced with a dilemma. Should she follow the path of duty or the path of love?

THE GOLDEN PUMA
Margaret Way

Catherine's time was spent looking after her father's Queensland farm. But what life was there without David, who wasn't interested in her?

WITH SOMEBODY ELSE
Theresa Charles

Rosamond sets off for Cornwall with Hugo to meet his family, blissfully unaware of the shocks in store for her.

A SUMMER FOR STRANGERS
Claire Hamilton

Because she had lost her job, her flat and she had no money, Tabitha agreed to pose as Adam's future wife although she believed the scheme to be deceitful and cruel.

VILLA OF SINGING WATER
Angela Petron

The disquieting incidents that occurred at the Vatican and the Colosseum did not trouble Jan at first, but then they became increasingly unpleasant and alarming.

CRUSADING NURSE
Jane Converse

It was handsome Dr. Corbett who opened Nurse Susan Leighton's eyes and who set her off on a lonely crusade against some powerful enemies and a shattering struggle against the man she loved.

WILD ENCHANTMENT
Christina Green

Rowan's agreeable new boss had a dream of creating a famous perfume using her precious Silverstar, but Rowan's plans were very different.

DESERT ROMANCE
Irene Ord

Sally agrees to take her sister Pam's place as La Chartreuse the dancer, but she finds out there is more to it than dyeing her hair red and looking like her sister.

HEART OF ICE
Marie Sidney

How was January to know that not only would the warmth of the Swiss people thaw out her frozen heart, but that she too would play her part in helping someone to live again?

LUCKY IN LOVE
Margaret Wood

Companion-secretary to wealthy gambler Laura Duxford, who lived in Monaco, seemed to Melanie a fabulous job. Especially as Melanie had already lost her heart to Laura's son, Julian.

NURSE TO PRINCESS JASMINE
Lilian Woodward

Nick's surgeon brother, Tom, performs an operation on an Arabian princess, and she invites Tom, Nick and his fiancé to Omander, where a web of deceit and intrigue closes about them.

THE WAYWARD HEART
Eileen Barry

Disaster-prone Katherine's nickname was "Kate Calamity", but her boss went too far with an outrageous proposal, which because of her latest disaster, she could not refuse.

FOUR WEEKS IN WINTER
Jane Donnelly

Tessa wasn't looking forward to meeting Paul Mellor again — she had made a fool of herself over him once before. But was Orme Jared's solution to her problem likely to be the right one?

SURGERY BY THE SEA
Sheila Douglas

Medical student Meg hadn't really wanted to go and work with a G.P. on the Welsh coast although the job had its compensations. But Owen Roberts was certainly not one of them!

HEAVEN IS HIGH
Anne Hampson

The new heir to the Manor of Marbeck had been found. But it was rather unfortunate that when he arrived unexpectedly he found an uninvited guest, complete with stetson and high boots.

LOVE WILL COME
Sarah Devon

June Baker's boss was not really her idea of her ideal man, but when she went from third typist to boss's secretary overnight she began to change her mind.

ESCAPE TO ROMANCE
Kay Winchester

Oliver and Jean first met on Swale Island. They were both trying to begin their lives afresh, but neither had bargained for complications from the past.

CASTLE IN THE SUN
Cora Mayne

Emma's invalid sister, Kym, needed a warm climate, and Emma jumped at the chance of a job on a Mediterranean island. But Emma soon finds that intrigues and hazards lurk on the sunlit isle.

BEWARE OF LOVE
Kay Winchester

Carol Brampton resumes her nursing career when her family is killed in a car accident. With Dr. Patrick Farrell she begins to pick up the pieces of her life, but is bitterly hurt when insinuations are made about her to Patrick.

DARLING REBEL
Sarah Devon

When Jason Farradale's secretary met with an accident, her glamorous stand-in was quite unable to deal with one problem in particular.